THE
GIANTS
AND
THE
JONESES

Also by
JULIA DONALDSON
FROM EGMONT

Night Monkey Day Monkey

Follow the Swallow

Spinderella

The Wrong Kind of Bark

The Quick Brown Fox Club

FOR OLDER READERS

Running on the Cracks

THE GIANTS AND THE JONESES

JULIA DONALDSON

Illustrations by Paul Hess

EGMONT

EGMONT

We bring stories to life

First published in Great Britain 2004
by Egmont UK Limited
The Yellow Building, 1 Nicholas Road
London, W11 4AN

This edition published 2017

Text copyright © 2004 Julia Donaldson 2004
Cover illustration copyright © 2017 Erika Meza
Interior illustrations copyright © 2004 Paul Hess

The moral rights of the author and illustrators have been asserted

ISBN 978 1 4052 0760 7

www.egmont.co.uk

A CIP catalogue record for this title is available from the
British Library

Typeset by Avon DataSet Ltd, Bidford on Avon B50 4JH
Printed and bound in Great Britain by the CPI Group

42203/14

All rights reserved. No part of this publication may be reproduced,
stored ina retrieval system, or transmitted, in any form or by any means,
electronic,mechanical, photocopying, recording or otherwise,
without the prior permission of the publisher and copyright owner.

Stay safe online. Any website addresses listed in this book are correct at
the time of going to print. However, Egmont is not responsible for content
hosted by third parties. Please be aware that online content can be subject to
change and websites can contain content that is unsuitable for children.
We advise that all children are supervised when using the internet.

MIX
Paper
FSC FSC® C018306

For

Angharad and Rhiannon

Contents

1   The secret box 1

2   Throg 5

3   Snail number nineteen 8

4   Bimplestonk 13

5   In the bag 19

6   Suspicion and sandwiches 25

7   The mountain of cliffs 28

8   Weedkiller 38

9   Snishsnosh 41

10 Discovery 51

11 The return of Zab 56

12 The staircase and the slide 63

13 Whackleclack 67

14 The icy lake 71

15 Oggle arump 79

16 The battle jar 82

17 Sweefswoof 94

18 The running-away collection 98

19 Spratchkin 105

20 The monster on the bed 109

21 Blood 120

22 Alone 126

23 Beely bobbaleely 131

24 The bridge of doom 136

25 Escape 146

26 The spy 156

27 Nug! 161

28 Over the edge 166

29 Oidle oy 173

30 Unpicking the stitches 178

31 Three years later 187

English/Groilish dictionary 191

Groilish/English dictionary 195

The secret box

'BEESH, BEESH, BEESH!' said the girl giant. In giant language, this meant, 'Please, please, please!'

The girl giant, Jumbeelia, was sitting up in bed and holding out a book to her mother. 'Boooh, boooh, boooh, Mij!' she pleaded again.

Mij, Jumbeelia's mother, sighed. Without even looking at the book, she knew that the picture on the front was of a tiny little man standing on a leaf. When

· 1 ·

would Jumbeelia, who was nearly nine and perfectly capable of reading to herself, grow out of these babyish bedtime stories about the iggly plops?

Everyone knew that the iggly plops didn't really exist. Just as well, since they were such nasty little things in all the stories about them. Jumbeelia's big brother had stopped believing in them long before he was this age.

Jumbeelia's mother took a different book from the shelf. It had a picture of some nice normal giant children running about in school uniform.

But Jumbeelia looked so disappointed that Mij gave in. Yet again she told the ridiculous tale of the iggly plop who climbed up a bimplestonk and arrived in the land of Groil.

He was a very wicked iggly plop: he stole a hen and a harp and a lot of money. The poor giant who had been burgled chased after him but he wasn't fast enough; when he was halfway down the bimplestonk the iggly plop chopped it down and the giant fell to his death.

It was a horrible story, Mij thought. What was especially awful was the fact that the nasty iggly plop got away with his crimes instead of being punished. But Jumbeelia didn't seem to mind that. If anything she was on the iggly plop's side, and when her mother finished the story she wanted it all over again. 'Tweeko! Tweeko!' she cried.

Her mother refused, so Jumbeelia contented herself with asking questions about the iggly plops. Were they very *very* iggly? Would they reach up to her knee or were they as iggly as her iggly finger? Did they have iggly houses and trees and animals and beds and cups and spoons? And what did they eat, apart from bimples? They must eat bimples, because they climbed up bimplestonks.

But Mij wasn't much help. They *didn't* eat bimples and they *didn't* climb up bimplestonks, she said. How could they, when they didn't exist?

She kissed her daughter goodnight and switched out the bedside light.

As soon as the footsteps had died away, Jumbeelia switched the light back on. She got out of bed and weaved her way across her bedroom. She didn't walk in a straight line because her bedroom floor was covered in all her collections. There was a tin of coins, a bag of shells and a basket of fir cones. There was a heap of buttons, a hill of egg boxes and a mountain of cushions. But Jumbeelia didn't want to play with any of these things. She weaved her way round them all to the corner of the room and rummaged inside a big chest.

Was it still in here? Yes!

Jumbeelia took an old box out of the chest. It was made of different shapes of coloured wood. She shook it, and smiled when she heard the lovely dull rattling sound.

Turning the box over, she found the special shape she was looking for. It was a red diamond. She pressed it hard with her thumb, and the hidden drawer in the box sprang open.

Jumbeelia's smile grew and she put the box down on the floor. Squatting, she scooped up a handful of the lovely, wrinkly, squirly-patterned things inside.

'Bimples!' she murmured as she poured them from one hand to the other and back again.

And then an idea struck her – a wonderful, marvellous idea.

'Bimplestonk?' she said.

Throg

ALTHOUGH JUMBEELIA'S MOTHER was always telling
her that no grown-up giants believed in the iggly
plops, this wasn't quite true. There was one very old
giant who *did* believe in them, but no one took him
seriously because he talked to himself all the time. He
talked in rhyme about iggly plops and bimplestonks,
and as he talked he walked – not just anywhere but
round and round the very edge of Groil, the other side
of the wall, where the land stopped and the clouds

began. In his hand he carried a can full of extremely powerful weedkiller.

The old giant's name was Throg, which meant warning in giant language, and his rhymes *were* a warning to anyone who would listen – a warning that one day a new bimplestonk would spring up and that the wicked cunning iggly plops would climb up it and invade Groil.

Throg's favourite rhyme went like this:

Arump o chay ee glay, glay,   *(Around the land I go, go,*
Arump o chay ee glay.   *Around the land I go.*
Oy frikely frikely   *You horrible horrible*
bimplestonk,   *beanstalk,*
Eel kraggle oy flisterflay.   *I'll kill you soon.)*

Hardly anyone *did* listen to the old giant because most of the other giants preferred to stay away from the edge of Groil, fearing that they might fall off. But now and again one of Throg's rhymes would drift to them on the wind. Then they would shake their heads, smile, and call him a poor old man – 'Roopy floopy plop'.

Jumbeelia's father was a policeman. He had told her that Throg was forever calling at the police station and asking them to organise proper police patrols of the edgeland. But none of the police took this idea seriously. 'Roopy floopy plop,' they would say, just like all the other grown-up giants.

Jumbeelia had never been to the edgeland; she wasn't allowed the other side of the wall. But she had heard old Throg's rhymes, and now and then she caught sight of him taking a nap or eating sandwiches in a field. She would have liked to talk to him – to ask him what he knew about iggly plops and bimplestonks – but she didn't dare. She couldn't help feeling a little scared of him.

Snail number nineteen

DOWN IN THE land of the iggly plops, an eleven-year-old human boy called Stephen Jones lay sprawled on a garden path, surrounded by marbles.

'You stupid stick insect!' he yelled.

Stephen's sister Colette turned round from the flower bed where she had just picked a snail off a leaf. 'It's not a stick insect. It's a snail,' she said.

'I mean *you*, you brainless bluebottle!' Stephen scrambled to his feet and hurled a handful of marbles into a bush.

'Stop!' cried Colette. 'That's my marble collection!'

'I know it's your stupid marble collection,' said Stephen. 'I've just trodden on one, haven't I? Now *I'm* going to have a collection – a collection of bruises.'

'Sorry,' said Colette. 'But they're not stupid. They're beautiful. They're lovely and shiny and swirly.'

Stephen put on the silly high-pitched voice he used to imitate Colette. 'Lovely and shiny and swirly!' he screeched.

'Just because you can't appreciate anything that hasn't got an engine,' said Colette. She put the snail into the cardboard box at her feet and turned her back on Stephen. Another snail was sitting on a leaf, waving its horns around. Snail number nineteen, it was. 'In you go,' she said.

The other eighteen snails were sliding around in a slow bewildered way. They weren't taking much notice of the selection of leaves Colette had put in for them. Snail number four had climbed up the wall of the box and was nearly at the top.

'I'll have to make you a lid,' Colette told them.

'With holes in, so you can breathe.'

A bit of cardboard from her junk collection should do the trick. Colette took the box inside the house.

'Stupid centipede!' Stephen called after her, but half-heartedly. He had recovered from his fall and was now sitting on the seat of the lawn mower, fiddling with the controls. The lawn mower was brand new. It was gleaming and enormous. It even had a trailer. For Stephen it had been love at first sight.

As soon as she stepped into the house Colette heard Dad's voice.

'The basin is full of stamps!' he shouted.

She put the snail box on the kitchen table and ran up the first flight of stairs. Dad was standing in the bathroom doorway looking fed up.

'I'm sorry,' said Colette. 'I'm just soaking them off their envelopes. Can't you wash your hands in the kitchen?'

As Dad opened his mouth to reply a feather fell on his nose.

'Bird flying!' came another voice, from above them. Colette looked up. Her little sister Poppy was lying on her tummy on the top landing, throwing feathers down between the railings of the banisters.

'Stop! That's my feather collection! You're such a pest, Poppy!' Colette ran on up, her footsteps loud and furious.

But even louder and more furious was the voice which now rang up the stairs.

'Colette! Come here! *Now*!' It was Mum.

Colette grabbed Poppy's fistful of feathers and slunk back downstairs, past Dad who was still muttering about stamps. She opened the kitchen door.

'*Look* at them! They're everywhere!' Mum pointed at the table. The snails were slithering around among the crumbs from teatime, leaving slimy trails behind them. One had reached the rim of a jar of honey and an even more adventurous one (number four again) was climbing up the spout of the teapot.

'I'm sorry,' said Colette yet again. She put the feathers down and started to pick up the snails and put them back in the box. 'I was going to make them a lid but . . .'

But Mum didn't want to hear any buts. 'This is one collection too many,' she said. 'Put them back outside. *Now.*'

'Birds!' said Poppy, coming into the kitchen and spotting the feathers on the table. But Colette's big box was even more interesting. Poppy trailed after sister and box, out into the garden.

'Don't start collecting anything else out there, whatever you do!' Mum called after them.

And Colette didn't. Not that day, anyway. But this wasn't because she was obeying her mother. It was because she was about to be collected herself.

Bimplestonk

FOR THE SECOND time in her life, the girl giant climbed over the wall. Then she turned and looked back down the narrow road. She couldn't see far because of the mist, but she didn't think anyone was following her.

Thank goodness her horrible spying, prying brother Zab was safely away at boarding school.

No one had seen Jumbeelia yesterday, either, when she came this way and threw the bimple off the edge of

Groil. No one had heard her urging it to grow: 'Eep, bimple, eep!' At least, she didn't think so. But what about old Throg? Could he have been lurking around somewhere? Was he here now, hidden behind one of the huge boulders which she could only just make out through the mist?

It was Throg's rhymes, as well as the bedtime stories about the iggly plops, which had brought Jumbeelia here, but she certainly didn't want to bump into the strange old man.

She shivered. The air was colder today, and the mist grew thicker with every step she took. Soon she could hardly see anything – not even her hand when she held it out in front of her, not even her feet as they shuffled along the hard ground.

There wouldn't have been much to see anyway. No trees grew here in the cloudy edgeland; no flowers, no grass, nothing at all. The rocky ground was bare and smooth, even a little slippery.

It wouldn't do to slip – not so near the edge of Groil. Jumbeelia shuffled slowly, feeling with her feet for the place where the ground stopped and the emptiness began . . . the emptiness which she hoped would not after all be quite empty.

Here it was, sooner than she remembered. She stopped. And yes! Surely there *was* something looming out of the mist.

'Bimplestonk!' she murmured, full of wonder.

Jumbeelia reached out. She didn't have to reach far. Almost immediately her fingers touched something damp and cool and floppy – a leaf! And now her hand was curling round a thick firm stalk.

It was the loveliest thing she had ever seen or felt.

'Beely beely bimplestonk!'

So it was true! A bimple could grow into a bimplestonk overnight. And if that was true, surely the rest of the story must be true! Jumbeelia reached out with the other hand. And then her feet followed her hands . . .

Down she climbed. 'Boff, boff, boff!' Down, down, down through the clouds. Down, down, down to the land of the iggly plops. And when she was out of the clouds she could see it spread out below her, a patchwork of iggly green fields, with darker green blobs which must be woods, and threads of cotton which must be roads.

Of course, things always looked iggly from a distance. Maybe when she reached the ground everything would be the same size as in Groil.

But no! Here she was at the very bottom of the bimplestonk. She unclasped her hands and stepped out on to grass as short and fine as giant eyelashes. 'Iggly strimp!' she cried.

And then she noticed something much more wonderful. A few strides away, nibbling at the strimp, were some woolly creatures the size of mice. But they weren't mice, of course — they must be sheep.

'Iggly blebbers!'

Jumbeelia took her collecting bag off her back. It wasn't a very big bag but it had several pockets. She picked up one of the blebbers. It wriggled and bleated as she put it gently into one of the pockets. She put in a few tufts of strimp too, hoping that the blebber would settle down and eat them.

Excitement bubbled up inside her. Where there were blebbers there were bound to be plops.

She made her way across a few fields, stepping over the ankle-high hedges and splashing through a pond as shallow as a puddle.

She strode along a lane and came to a pillar box.

'Iggly pobo!' She picked it up and thrust it into a pocket of the bag.

She turned a corner and saw a telephone box.

'Iggly frangle!' she cried as it went into another pocket.

Round the next corner was something even better – a cluster of iggly houses. She couldn't see any plops, but in the nearest garden was a swinging seat covered in cushions.

'Iggly squodgies!' Into the bag they went. They would make a nice soft floor for the iggly plops. Surely, *surely* she would find some iggly plops soon.

But the other gardens were disappointingly empty, and though she peered in through the windows of the houses and saw lots of sweet iggly furniture there was not an iggly plop to be seen.

Jumbeelia began to worry that Mij would have woken up from her afternoon nap and be missing her.

Maybe she should go home and come back another day. After all, she had plenty of other iggly things to play with – the pobo, the frangle, the squodgies and, best of all, the beely woolly blebber. The blebber had stopped bleating and she could hear it munching the iggly strimp. She couldn't wait to offer it some proper giant-size strimp.

She was about to turn around when she noticed another house on its own about half a mile down the lane.

Ten strides and she was there. The front garden was empty, but when she saw what was in the back garden she gave an excited skip which set the blebber bleating all over again.

A machine was sitting in the middle of the lawn. 'Iggly strimpchogger,' she whispered in delight.

But even more exciting were the three creatures she could see – one of them in the seat of the strimpchogger, the other two nearby, bent over an iggly cardboard box.

Jumbeelia counted to herself: 'Wunk, twunk, thrink iggly plops!'

In the bag

'WHERE ARE WE?' Stephen's voice sounded shaky and his face was white.

Colette looked round at the blue canvas walls of their prison. She shuddered, remembering the fat pink tentacles that had put her there.

'I think we're in a giant's bag,' she whispered back.

'Don't talk rubbish – giants don't exist.'

But the next second they heard a deafening voice.

'Beely iggly plop,' it said, and the tentacles appeared

above them, with Poppy in their grip.

Poppy was laughing. 'Big girl do it 'gain,' she said as the giant hand released her. She seemed to think this was some new kind of glorious fairground ride.

'It's not a girl, it's a giant, silly,' Stephen snapped at her. 'It's probably going to eat us.'

But Poppy just repeated, 'Big girl,' and started bouncing on the cushions which covered the floor of the bag.

And then the canvas ceiling came down.

'All dark,' complained Poppy.

Colette felt sick with fear, but she managed to find her voice, and shouted, 'Stop! Let us out! Let us *out*!'

'It can't understand you. Didn't you hear it? It speaks a different language.' Stephen sounded angry, as if the whole thing was her fault.

A tremendous jolt threw them up into the air and down again. As the three of them rolled helplessly about on the cushions, Poppy giggled again. But Colette and Stephen were silent. They both knew what was happening. The giant was on the move.

'Mum! Dad! Help!' yelled Colette, but without much hope.

A sudden swoop and a bump, and the jolting stopped. Their dark ceiling was off again, and light streamed in.

'Maybe it's going to put us back?' said Colette.

'Maybe it's hungry,' said Stephen.

The hand came down – but not to take them out.

'It's putting something in,' said Colette.

'Peggy line!' said Poppy.

'Iggly swisheroo!' said the voice.

'Can't *anyone* round here speak English?' said Stephen. 'It's a washing line.'

And so it was – quite a long one, complete with pegged-out clothes, towels and sheets. A sheet landed on top of Colette and by the time she had struggled free the bag was dark and the bumpy journey had begun again.

Poppy, delighted with this new and grown-up toy, started unpegging the clothes and hoarding the pegs in a corner of the bag.

'Oh no, not you too,' said Stephen in disgust. 'Isn't one collector in this family enough?'

Colette turned on him. 'Do shut up,' she said. 'Can't you *ever* stop complaining?'

'Yes,' said Stephen triumphantly. 'I'll stop complaining when you stop collecting.'

Colette could hardly believe this. Here they were, jogging along in the dark, inside a giant's bag, and yet they were still squabbling.

Before she could think of a cutting retort, there was a terrifyingly loud noise right in her ear – a long, low grating kind of noise which seemed to come from within the bag itself. Colette found herself clutching Stephen despite their quarrel.

'What was that?' she said.

'Baa Lamb,' said Poppy.

'This isn't the time of year for lambs,' said Stephen in his Mr Know-All voice. 'Anyway, its bleat is too low-sounding. It's a sheep.'

As if in agreement the low bleating was repeated. It was just behind one of the canvas walls.

'Big girl got Baa Lamb,' said Poppy stubbornly.

'Big girl got great enormous sheep, you mean,' said Stephen. 'Probably for supper. Or maybe we're supper and the sheep is breakfast.'

Poppy started to cry then. Colette put an arm round her. 'Well done, Stephen,' she said.

'I'm sorry. I'm sorry, Poppy,' said Stephen, who hardly ever apologised. Colette noticed that his voice was shaking again. 'I just wish I could get us out of here . . . I know! Give me one of those clothes pegs, Poppy.'

Poppy sniffed and handed him one. Stephen started picking away with it at a corner of the bag as they jolted along.

'What are you doing?' asked Colette.

'I can feel a little hole here, where the stitching has come loose. If I can make it bigger maybe we can escape.'

'But we'd get killed jumping.'

'She might put the bag down again,' said Stephen, still hacking away. 'There – it's big enough to look through, at least.' He lay on his tummy and put his eye to the hole.

'Oh no,' he said.

'What is it?' asked Colette.

'You'd better have a look.'

So Colette looked through the hole and was overcome with dizziness and fear.

'Is it what I think it is?' she said.

'Yes. We're going up a beanstalk.'

Suspicion and sandwiches

Arump o chay ee glay, glay,
Arump o chay ee glay.
Oy frikely frikely himplestonk
Eel kraggle oy flisterflay.

OLD THROG HOBBLED along, reciting his favourite rhyme and swinging his can of weedkiller in one hand and his sandwich bag in the other. His voice was faint and cracked, and he felt tired and cold. The mist was thicker than usual today, so thick that it might be difficult to make out a bimplestonk if one had eeped up during the month or so since he had last walked along this stretch of the edgeland.

It was time for his afternoon nap, Throg decided. He climbed over the wall, emerging out of the edgeland mist into a sunny field. It was good to warm his old bones, eat a sandwich and doze off for a few minutes, but he knew that his dreams would be troubled, as they always were. What if the bimplestonk appeared and the iggly plop invasion took place while he was asleep?

Throg woke with a start. Someone really *was* coming, he sensed it in his bones.

It was all right. It was just a girl, with a bag on her back. Throg recognised her as the daughter of one of the useless policemen who refused to take the iggly plop invasion seriously.

The girl was walking along the narrow road which ran from the edgeland towards the main town. What had she been doing all by herself so near the emptiness?

'Wahoy!' he called out to her in his thin old voice,

but the girl didn't seem to hear his greeting. She continued on her way, and Throg noticed that she had a huge grin on her face.

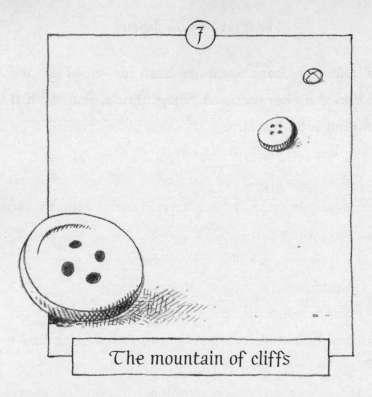

The mountain of cliffs

'T IS IS THE last button,' said Colette. She pushed it
through the hole in the floor of the bag.

Stephen had scoffed when she had emptied her
pockets and produced the buttons – yet another useless
collection as far as he could see. But when Colette
suggested leaving a trail of buttons, so that they could
find their way back to the top of the beanstalk, he had
grudgingly admitted this wasn't a bad idea.

'I think we've arrived,' he said now, with his eye to

the hole in the bag. 'She's opening a door.'

And that was when they heard the second voice. It was even louder than the first one. It sounded angry, and it went on and on and on.

Their kidnapper's voice sounded a lot quieter now. 'Yimp, yimp, yimp,' it kept saying, in reply to the deafening jumble of furious sounds.

'Big girl got cross Mummy,' whispered Poppy.

Colette realised she was probably right.

'I wonder what she's cross *about*?' she whispered back.

'Maybe because her precious little daughter hasn't collected enough food for supper,' said Stephen.

At last, after yet another apologetic sounding 'yimp' from the girl giant, the mother giant fell silent and the children were on the move again.

'We're in a house,' hissed Stephen.

Colette heard a door open, and then her stomach lurched as they were plunged to the ground.

'This is it,' said Stephen. He was brandishing a clothes peg.

Colette picked one up too. It didn't feel like a very powerful weapon.

The ceiling came off the bag.

'Come on, Poppy, get ready to fight!' ordered Stephen.

But Poppy stretched out her arms. 'Big girl 'gain!' she said, as the enormous fingers curled round her.

'Stop! Don't you hurt my sister!' shouted Stephen.

He lunged out at one of the fingers with his clothes peg. But the hand – with Poppy in it – was already too high to reach.

Colette gazed up helplessly and saw a giant face looking down.

'Beely iggly plop,' said the giant, lifting Poppy towards her mouth . . .

'No!' Stephen bellowed, and he hurled the peg at the giant. It hit her cheek, but she didn't seem to notice. Her mouth was touching Poppy now. Soon it would be opening.

But it didn't open. Instead, a sort of sucking, smacking noise came from it.

'All wet!' said Poppy.

'Yuk!' said Stephen. 'Was that a kiss?'

Before Colette could answer, it was her turn. She was lifted up and brought towards the shining pink lips. She closed her eyes. The next second she felt a dampness all over her cheek and an explosion in her ear.

She dared herself to open her eyes, and caught a glimpse of a hairy nostril before she was lowered again and pushed through a door.

'Beely jum,' boomed the giant.

Colette found herself in a sitting room. To her surprise, the furniture was more or less human-size. There was a sofa, two armchairs, one of them on its side, and an upside-down table.

'Boo!'

Colette jumped as a figure flung itself at her from behind one of the armchairs. It was Poppy.

A second later Stephen was thrust in beside them, an expression of disgust on his face.

'Yuk!' he said again. He never had been a great fan of kisses.

'At least it's better than being eaten,' Colette pointed out.

And then, 'Baa Lamb!' shrieked Poppy.

A big and rather tatty-looking sheep with magnificent

twisty horns had joined them and was eyeing them suspiciously.

Stephen rolled his eyes. 'Of all the animals in the world to be stuck with!' he said.

At that moment, the wall with the door in it began to move. It swung right away from them, revealing the girl giant's huge grinning face.

'Jumbeelia,' she said, pointing to herself.

'What a stupid name,' muttered Stephen.

'Jumbeelia! JUMBEELIA!' the giant mother called from a distance. She sounded impatient rather than angry.

'Ootle rootle!' their kidnapper yelled in reply, and the front wall of the doll's house slid back into place.

For a second Jumbeelia's shiny giant lips appeared at their window, with a single finger over them. 'Sshh!' she whispered. Then she was gone.

'Now's our chance,' said Stephen.

'For what?' asked Colette.

'To get away, of course.' He was already at the door of the doll's house.

But Poppy was trying to make friends with the

sheep. 'Nice Baa Lamb,' she kept saying as she chased it round and round the room.

The sheep, who seemed to be keener to escape from Poppy than from Giant Land, lowered its horns and pushed a door open. It went through, with Poppy still in pursuit.

'Look – there's a kitchen,' said Colette, following her.

'Never mind that. Just get Poppy and *come*!' Stephen urged.

Colette ignored him. She was inspecting the cooker. 'The knobs won't turn,' she said.

Stephen sighed. 'Okay, *I'll* get Poppy,' he said.

Colette looked inside the fridge. It wasn't at all cold, and the food on the shelves was made of plastic. Suddenly she felt hungry.

'What are we supposed to eat?' she asked.

'I keep telling you – it's them that does the eating, not us!' said Stephen, grabbing Poppy's arm. 'We've got to get away from here!'

Colette saw the desperation in his eyes and her own fear flooded back.

'You're right, Stephen,' she said. 'Come on, Poppy.'

In any case, the sheep was now leading the way. The children followed it back through the main room of the doll's house and out of the front door.

'Grass!' said Poppy. But it wasn't grass. It felt more like very deep thick velvety moss. Their feet sank into it as they walked.

'It's a carpet, stupid,' said Stephen. Then, 'Hey, look at that!' and he pointed at a huge heap of cars, buses and lorries. He prodded an ambulance.

'It's plastic,' he said, disappointed. 'They're just a load of toys.'

Colette didn't answer him. She was more interested in another heap of objects which looked like big wrinkly pale green bowls.

'Hat!' said Poppy, putting one on her head. It had a little stalk coming out of the middle of it.

'They're acorn cups!' exclaimed Colette.

'She's completely mad,' said Stephen.

'No, she's not mad,' said Colette thoughtfully. 'I think she must like collecting things – just like me.'

'Yes, mad, like I said,' said Stephen.

'Oh shut up! Look, I can see the door. And it's open!'

It wasn't easy making their way across the furry green carpet towards the giant door. First they had to climb over giant pencils which lay like fallen trees, and then they found their way blocked by an enormous pile of what looked like shiny coloured plates.

'I think they're buttons,' said Colette.

'Trust her,' said Stephen.

Colette found herself springing to the girl giant's defence. 'You shouldn't groan like that. Look how useful *my* button collection was.'

'Oh yeah?' said Stephen in his most infuriating voice.

Colette turned on him. 'What's the matter with you, Stephen Jones? Why do you have to be so scornful all the time? Don't you want to get home? Don't you want to see Mum and Dad again?'

'That's great coming from you. Who wanted to stay and explore the doll's house?'

'There you go again! Can't you see, we're all in this together? We'll never get home if you keep getting at me.'

'It's you that's getting at *me*!'

'Hill all slidey!' called out Poppy, interrupting their quarrel. She was trying to climb the button hill, and laughing as the buttons slithered and clattered under her weight.

'We need to go *round* it, not over it,' Colette told her. She turned to Stephen. 'Coming?'

Stephen shrugged sulkily, but followed her round the hill of buttons. After that the going was a little easier. A bright yellow plastic railway track led them nearly all the way to the door, and when it stopped abruptly there was only one more hill in their way – a soft hairy purple one. 'It's a towel,' said Colette.

Then, 'Big red field,' said Poppy.

'It does look like one.' Colette gazed across the new empty space. 'But look at those railings over there – I've never seen a field with a fence that high.'

Stephen still said nothing. Colette touched his arm gently, trying to make up, but he shrugged her off.

They made their way towards the wooden railings, past another giant door. The red carpet was thinner than the green one, less squashy to walk on.

Colette's spirits rose. In her mind they were already

out of the house and following the trail of buttons to the top of the beanstalk.

'I bet Mum and Dad won't be expecting us back so soon,' she said.

But then, 'Cliff,' said Poppy, and they all stopped.

Colette looked down. Below them the red ground dropped away steeply. They were indeed at the top of a cliff, twice her own height – too tall to jump down, and too steep to climb down.

Of course. The towering wooden railings were banisters. The cliff was a giant stair. And below it was another stair, and another one and another one.

The giant staircase was a mountain of cliffs.

8

Weedkiller

IT WAS TIME for Throg to be on his way – back over the wall, back to his patrol. The edgeland mist had thinned during his doze, and it wasn't quite so cold. Throg felt refreshed and cheerful. When he was in a good mood he sometimes made up a tune for his favourite rhyme, and he did so now as he tottered along once more, straining his eyes to peer out into the emptiness.

Arump o chay ee glay, glay,
Arump o chay ee glay.
Oy frikely frikely bimplestonk,
Eel kraggle oy flisterflay.

His voice felt stronger now, after his sleep, and he was enjoying the sound of it. He screwed up his eyes and flung back his head, singing full-belt, his hobble almost transformed into a stride.

He had nearly sung the song through three times when his foot slipped and he landed with a bump on his bottom.

He sat there for a moment, cursing the slippery ground but most of all himself. There was no excuse for such carelessness, especially with the mist thinner than usual. So thin that he could clearly see the edge of the land. So thin that he could clearly see . . .

'O bimplestonk!' Throg was on his feet in a flash. Yes, there it was, exactly the same as in all the pictures – the frikely thick stalk, the frikely green leaves and the frikely green pods which he knew were full of bimples.

Old Throg's heart thumped as he peered down.

He couldn't see far, because of the cloud, but there was no sign of any iggly plops.

So this was it. The moment he had waited for all his life.

Throg picked up the can of weedkiller. He unscrewed the lid, then leant carefully forwards and sloshed some of the powerful liquid on to the top leaf.

The bimplestonk began to shrivel.

9

Snishsnosh

'CAN'T YOU STOP Poppy bouncing?' Stephen said to Colette. 'It's getting on my nerves.'

'Bouncing's better than moaning,' replied Colette, ~~secretly smiling to herself because Stephen was talking~~ to her again.

They were back in the doll's house, where they had discovered a bedroom at the top of a flight of stairs. There were two plastic beds and a giant sardine tin. Inside the sardine tin were the cushions from the swing, and Poppy – the only cheerful one – was jumping up and down on them.

'Why did we have to come back here?' Stephen sat on one of the beds, his head in his hands.

'You *know* why,' Colette reminded him. 'It's best if Jumbeelia doesn't realise we tried to escape.'

As if on cue they heard giant footsteps and Jumbeelia's voice. 'Snishsnosh!' she said.

She lifted the front off the doll's house and started to fiddle about in the kitchen. Poppy ran down the stairs. Colette and Stephen followed more slowly.

On the kitchen table was an object which looked a bit like a very long loaf of bread. But it wasn't crusty like bread; it was smooth, and slightly greasy-looking, and yellowish. A faint trail of steam was rising from it, and the smell was definitely *not* one of bread. Yet it was a smell that Colette knew very well, one of her favourite smells in fact, a mixture of salt and vinegar and . . .

'Nice big chip,' said Poppy.

'It's the biggest chip in the world!' said Stephen, suddenly in a good mood, and Colette laughed.

'Snishsnosh!' said Jumbeelia again. Colette's hunger

became a sharp pang now that she realised what the delicious smell was.

The girl giant began to cut the chip into slices.

'Watch it,' said Stephen. 'That's a giant razor blade. She could be planning to carve *us* up with it.' But when Jumbeelia handed out slices of the giant chip, he bit into his straight away.

'This beats McDonald's,' he said.

'It's lucky she likes the same things as us, isn't it?' said Colette between mouthfuls. 'Supposing they ate slug dumplings or something?'

'Don't speak too soon – what's this?'

The girl giant had put three round dark objects on the table. They looked a bit like bun-size Christmas puddings. Colette sniffed one, then nibbled at it. It tasted familiar.

'Nice big raisin,' said Poppy.

As they munched away, Jumbeelia placed something else in front of them. It was a tube of toothpaste longer than the tabletop.

'Trust her to think we want to eat *toothpaste*,' said Stephen.

'Maybe she wants to clean our teeth,' said Colette.

They were both wrong. Jumbeelia unscrewed the lid of the tube. To the children this was the size of a large vase. She poured a few orange-coloured drops into it from a giant bottle. 'Beely gloosh,' she said.

They let Jumbeelia hold the toothpaste lid to their lips and tilt it while they sipped, and only a little of the drink trickled down their chins.

'It had better not be poison,' muttered Stephen.

'Don't be silly – it's orange juice,' said Colette. 'But what's she got now?'

'Peggy line!' cried Poppy, recognising the washing line that had been in the bag with them.

'Iggly swisheroo,' said Jumbeelia.

She picked up Poppy and took off her jumper.

'All cold,' complained Poppy as her skirt came off too, and, 'Not bedtime,' when Jumbeelia dressed her in a long lacy nighty. But she was delighted with the stripy football jumper which the giant girl then slipped over her head. 'All pretty now,' she said.

'It looks like it's your turn,' said Stephen to Colette, as Jumbeelia reached out for her.

Even though the girl giant was gentle in the way she handled them, Colette felt quite nervous.

'Just keep still and you'll be all right,' said Stephen.

Jumbeelia removed Colette's clothes and coaxed her arms into a fleecy-lined purple anorak and her legs into a pair of lime green Bermuda shorts.

Stephen hooted with laughter, until Jumbeelia picked him up and dressed him in a pink ballet dress with a sticking-out skirt.

Poppy clapped her hands and said, 'Stephen do dance!'

'Yes, come on, Stephen – up on your points!' said Colette, enjoying his outraged expression.

'I can't wear this,' he shouted. 'Give me some boys' clothes.'

But Jumbeelia couldn't understand him. In any case, she had a different plan.

Carefully, she lifted them up again, and put them down in a different part of the bedroom. The carpet here was strewn with life-size plastic farm animals, some of them upright, others lying forlornly on their sides.

Jumbeelia put Colette on a milking stool beside

a plastic cow. Colette realised she was supposed to milk it, but of course no milk came from its hard pink udder.

Poppy was allowed to sit on a big carthorse. She loved this and started making clip-clop noises.

Stephen had his eye on a tractor but instead Jumbeelia gave him a bucket.

'Stephen feed chickens,' said Poppy.

'I'm not throwing imaginary corn to plastic hens!' said Stephen in disgust, and he hurled the bucket away.

'Pecky iggly plop!' Jumbeelia was wagging her finger at Stephen and Colette was frightened that she might decide to punish him for his bad temper.

But a sudden bleating distracted the girl giant. There, among the plastic sheep, was the real one. It was looking more dishevelled than ever, with bits of green carpet fluff mixed up in its dirty wool.

'Iggly blebber!' cried Jumbeelia in delight.

'That's let me off the hook,' said Stephen.

'Yes, but don't annoy her again – you had me really worried,' said Colette.

Something else was worrying her too. It was the fact

that Jumbeelia seemed to have forgotten all about the sheep until it reappeared.

Jumbeelia picked up one of the plastic sheep and made it rub noses with the real one, as if to cheer it up. But it didn't stop bleating.

'Baa Lamb hungry,' said Poppy from her carthorse.

Jumbeelia seemed to have the same idea. She started to rummage about inside a huge bag.

'That's the bag *we* were in,' said Colette.

The girl giant produced a handful of normal-size grass from a pocket of the bag. Then she put something else down on the floor.

'Iggly li'angle,' she said.

'It's a phone box,' said Colette.

'I bet it's the one from the village!' said Stephen indignantly.

'Phone Mummy, phone Daddy,' said Poppy, and slithered off the horse's back.

Almost as if she understood, Jumbeelia opened the door of the phone box and popped her inside.

'Hello, Mummy, hello, Daddy. Come here,' Poppy said. Then her face crumpled. She dropped the telephone receiver and left it dangling.

Colette opened the door for her.

'Mummy, Daddy not there,' said Poppy.

'No,' said Colette miserably. The sight of the familiar phone box had brought back all her own homesickness.

'I expect Mum and Dad have found the beanstalk by now,' she told Poppy, trying to cheer her up. 'Or else the police have. Someone will come and rescue us soon. They're probably on their way now.'

Stephen turned on her. 'What? You want to just wait here playing farms with Jumbo till someone rescues us?'

'Well, you think of a way of getting down the stairs then.'

'Ssh!' said Jumbeelia, and the next second she had thrust them into the doll's-house bedroom. They heard her mother come into the room.

Colette put her finger to her lips, and Stephen nodded. Even Poppy seemed to understand that the giant woman was more of a threat than the girl. Without saying a word, she lay down on the cushions inside the sardine tin, with her thumb in her mouth. 'We might as well too,' whispered Colette, and she and Stephen lay down on the two beds.

Within seconds, Poppy's thumb had slipped from her mouth. She was asleep.

Colette lay awake. She didn't know if Stephen was awake too. She didn't dare whisper anything to him.

She felt very lonely as she lay there, half-listening to what she guessed must be a bedtime story being told in a droning voice by the giant mother. She tried not to think about her own mother and the three empty beds at home.

The light went off, and before long Colette heard a rumbling sound coming from the direction of Jumbeelia's bed.

'Jumbo's asleep,' whispered Stephen.

'I thought you were too!' answered Colette, relieved that he wasn't.

'I've just thought of it,' said Stephen.

'Of what?'

'A railway line.'

'What are you talking about?'

'You said to think of a way to get downstairs, and I have. Remember that plastic railway track near Jumbo's bedroom door? It's like the one I used to have – it's made of different sections that clip together. If we can unclip one we could use it as a slide to get from stair to stair.'

'That's not a bad idea, Mr Know-All,' admitted Colette.

'Let's do it, then.'

'What, now? But Poppy's asleep.'

'Well, let's try it out and then wake her up if it works.'

They tiptoed out of the doll's house, navigated their way to the railway track, and succeeded in unclipping one of the bright yellow sections. They were dragging it towards the door when an anguished, grating sound from under the bed made them jump.

'What was that?' whispered Colette.

The sound came again. It was loud enough to wake the whole house, and this time there was no mistaking it.

'Oh no,' moaned Stephen softly. 'Shut up, Baa Lamb!'

Discovery

JUMBEELIA'S MOTHER, MIJ, was pottering about her bedroom when she heard a noise.

She stood still and listened. Nothing, except for the annoying drip of the bathroom tap that wouldn't turn off properly.

Inside her, the bobbaleely kicked. He or she was already quite a lively character. Mij sat down on the bed and began thinking again about names. Woozly for a girl. (That meant cuddly.) If it was a boy, perhaps

Jinjarn – kind heart.

Not that her other children had lived up to their names, she reflected sadly. Her son's name, Zab, meant peace, but Zab was anything but peaceful. In fact, it was quite a relief when he was away at school. As for Jumbeelia, her name meant home-lover, but look how she had turned out! Her bedroom was always in a mess and she was forever wandering *away* from home, collecting yet more horrible dirty things.

Where had Jumbeelia been today? Mij was supposed to have a rest every afternoon – it was the doctor's orders – but how *could* she rest properly if her daughter was going to run off like that?

Maybe Jumbeelia felt lonely playing by herself in the house. It wouldn't help when Zab came home from school tomorrow; he wasn't much of a companion for her, more of a tormentor. And how would it be once the bobbaleely was born? What if Jumbeelia felt jealous and neglected? Then she might start wandering off even more.

Mij was no animal-lover, but she did sometimes wonder if she ought to get a pet for her daughter. Zab had had a bird once, a yellow canary which his grandmother had given him, but he had never cared for it much and didn't seem to miss it after it flew away when he left its cage open. Jumbeelia would surely be better at looking after a pet – or would she just lose interest in it? Her crazes always tended to wear off quite quickly.

Oh, children were such a worry!

Baaaa!

There it was again! The sound was coming from Jumbeelia's bedroom.

By the light from the landing Mij saw that Jumbeelia was fast asleep. She was snoring slightly, but the noise she had heard was definitely not a snore.

Mij glanced round the room. There was no sign of any intruder.

Crunch. She had trodden on something. It was almost impossible *not* to tread on something in her daughter's messy bedroom. She looked down to see what was underfoot this time. It was a section of plastic railway track.

And then something moved and she gasped.

There at her feet was a nasty-looking grubby little creature with horns. She took a step back, in horror.

Calm down, she told herself: it must be an iggly clockwork toy.

She forced herself to squat down and inspect it. The creature made the sound again, and she noticed that it was surrounded by little brown balls, like mouse droppings.

It wasn't a toy. It was alive!

It looked – but that was ridiculous, it couldn't be! – like a tiny sheep.

Whatever it was, it was disgusting and unhygienic, and must be disposed of without delay. Bracing herself, Mij trapped the revolting blebbery thing under an empty box. As she did so, she imagined she heard another sound, like a tiny gasp, coming from under Jumbeelia's bed.

She listened again but all was quiet.

Now wasn't the time to search the room, but in the morning she would force Jumbeelia to have a thorough clear-out.

Meanwhile, back to her unpleasant task. She

couldn't bring herself to touch the nasty iggly creature. Rummaging under the bed, she grasped a furry slipper. That should do the job . . .

Colette and Stephen watched helplessly from their hiding place under Jumbeelia's bed as the giant mother used the slipper to sweep the sheep into the box. They saw her carry it out of the room, closing the door behind her.

They heard footsteps, and more doors opening and closing, and then, a while later, the flushing of a giant toilet.

The return of Zab

Z AB PULLED JUMBEELIA'S favourite scrunchy off her
hair. When she tried to snatch it back he laughed.

He had only been home from boarding school for
half an hour and already he was being unbearable.

Mij had given them a mid-morning snack: two
packets of crisps and a bowl of cherries. Jumbeelia loved
cherries – not just eating them, but finding the pairs
with joined-together stalks and putting them over her
ears like earrings. But as soon as Zab saw her do that he

snatched them off and popped them in his mouth. He had already eaten most of her crisps as well as his own.

He was stretching and twanging the scrunchy now. Jumbeelia tried again to grab it from him but he held it above his head.

She called out to her parents: 'Mij! Pij!'

Pij, in his police uniform, popped his head round the door for a hurried 'yahaw' and to tell them not to fight. He was late for his shift and didn't have time to listen to Jumbeelia's protests.

Zab was quick to find a use for the scrunchy: as a catapult, to launch cherry stones at his sister.

Jumbeelia tried to escape from the kitchen, sneaking the last two cherries into her nearly empty crisp packet. She hoped the iggly plops would like them. But before she was out of the room Zab came after her and grabbed the crisp bag.

'Nug! Askorp!' Jumbeelia's shriek brought Mij to her rescue, but it was too late to retrieve the crisps and cherries: Zab had already eaten them.

Their mother did her soothing act. She said that Zab must just be tired after his long term and the journey home, and suggested that he had a sleep. Zab shrugged, and sloped off to his room.

He was such a lazy boy, Jumbeelia thought, but she certainly wasn't going to complain. Now she would be able to have some time on her own to play with the iggly plops; and to look for the iggly blebber, which had mysteriously disappeared during the night.

But Mij had other ideas. It was time, she announced, to tidy Jumbeelia's bedroom. They would do it together.

Usually Jumbeelia could wriggle out of this task by putting it off to the next day. 'Chingulay,' she would plead. 'Chingulay, Mij! Beesh, beesh, beesh!' and finally Mij would cave in.

But not today. Today Mij put her foot down. She propelled Jumbeelia into her bedroom, and there she told her about the disgusting little creature she had discovered during the night.

Jumbeelia gasped. 'O iggly blebber!'

Mij looked at her suspiciously. So Jumbeelia knew about the creature? In that case, where on earth had she found it?

Jumbeelia refused to say. Instead, she turned on Mij, distraught, demanding where the iggly blebber was now.

'Queesh? Queesh? QUEESH?' she shouted. But Mij didn't reply; she just kept picking stuff off the floor and stuffing it into boxes.

Now she was over by the doll's house. Any second and she might discover the iggly plops. Silently, Jumbeelia willed them to keep still.

Mij unhinged the front of the doll's house.

She picked up an armchair and put it the right way up. Then she clicked her tongue in disapproval as she found part of a snishsnosh on the kitchen table. She scolded Jumbeelia. There was lots of nice plastic food in the doll's-house fridge: why did she have to play with real food?

To Jumbeelia's relief, Mij moved away and started picking up pencils from the floor.

Jumbeelia peeped into the doll's house. At first she couldn't see the iggly plops but then she noticed a bit of pink ballet dress sticking out from under the sofa.

There they lay, the three of them, side by side, the iggliest one, the nice tame one, sandwiched between the wild girl and the wild boy. Good old iggly plops! They had learnt that her mother wasn't to be trusted.

By now Mij was putting away the farm animals, which reminded Jumbeelia about the iggly blebber.

'Queesh? Queesh? QUEESH?' she asked again. 'Queesh ez o iggly blebber?'

Mij still wouldn't tell her, but this time she was more sympathetic. If Jumbeelia would just stop making such a fuss, and clear up the railway lines instead, there would be two nice surprises for her.

Feeling excited now, Jumbeelia tidied up much faster, wondering all the time what the two surprises would be.

The room was beginning to look unrecognisably neat. Mij sat down on the bed and beckoned Jumbeelia to sit beside her.

The first surprise was that Grishmij would be coming to stay in a week's time.

'Grishmij! Beely Grishmij!' Jumbeelia clapped her hands. She loved her grandmother, who always seemed to have time for her. They would make blackberry jam together, and Jumbeelia could show off all her latest collections (though maybe not the iggly plops).

Mij explained the reason for Grishmij's visit. It was to do with the new bobbaleely. The doctor had said that Mij must go into hospital a week before the bobbaleely was due, so Grishmij was coming to help Pij look after Jumbeelia.

'Da Zab?'

'Nug.' Not Zab too. Zab was going to stay with Grishpij – the grandparents felt that the two children together would be too much of a handful.

This was even better news. To have Zab away from the house for a whole week of the holidays, with Grishmij all to herself!

But what was the second surprise?

Mij smiled, and asked Jumbeelia if she would like to have a pet.

'Iggly blebber?' asked Jumbeelia hopefully.

Mij shuddered at the thought. No, not a blebber, she said. A spratchkin. She had heard that a spratch on a nearby farm had had three spratchkins. They weren't quite ready to leave their mother yet, but Mij offered to take Jumbeelia to the farm now, to look at them and choose one.

'Iggly spratchkin!' Jumbeelia hugged Mij. For a moment she forgot all about the iggly blebber and about Zab.

She even forgot about the iggly plops.

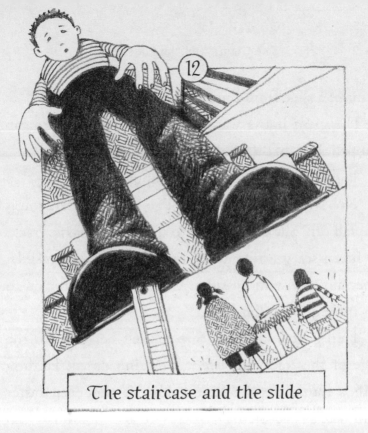

The staircase and the slide

'THEY'VE GONE OUT!' said Colette. 'That was the front door.'

Fortunately, Jumbeelia's bedroom door was open. And, fortunately, Jumbeelia's mother had not spotted the section of railway track which Colette and Stephen had left hidden under Jumbeelia's bed last night.

It was easy to drag the railway line out on to the landing, now that Jumbeelia's bedroom was so tidy. And, as Stephen had thought, it was just the right length to make a slide from the top stair to the one below.

The giant house was very quiet. Somewhere a tap dripped, but that was all.

'Poppy go down slide,' said Poppy.

'No. Wait,' said Colette. 'I'll go first, to catch you if you fall off.' She climbed on to the yellow plastic track.

It was scary sitting at the top of a such a steep slide, especially one with no sides. Colette turned over on to her tummy. That felt safer.

'Here I go!' she said. She relaxed her grip on the edge of the track and went whizzing down, landing with a bump on the stair below. It was even faster than she'd expected. Colette looked anxiously up at Poppy.

'Don't forget to keep holding on!' she called.

Poppy slid down safely, though she complained that the track was 'all bumpy'. Stephen followed.

They had managed the first stair, and the others should be just the same.

'I hope there aren't too many,' said Colette.

After three stairs, Poppy started clamouring for Baa Lamb.

'Baa Lamb isn't coming. He likes it in Jumbeelia's bedroom.' Colette didn't like lying to Poppy, but she felt that the truth would be too frightening for her little sister. The sight of the giant mother sweeping the sheep into a box and the sound of the giant toilet flushing had stayed with Colette all morning. She wished it had been a bad dream, but she knew that it had really happened. And it could happen to them too.

Slide, bump; slide, bump; slide, bump. They were into a rhythm now with the railway track; they knew exactly what to do and hardly needed to talk to each other any more.

They rounded the bend in the stairs and had a view of the hall below. So very *far* below! Colette felt suddenly tired. Would this never end?

The dripping tap was above them now, and somewhere below they heard a clock ticking the seconds away.

'Let's hope we make it before Jumbo and her Mumbo get back,' said Stephen.

Colette had just reached the next stair when she heard a door open.

She turned round and froze. On the step above her Stephen and Poppy froze too.

Someone was coming down the stairs towards them. There was nowhere to hide.

And now, an enormous boy was standing above them . . . bending down . . . picking them up, not gently the way Jumbeelia did, but grabbing them roughly, Stephen and Poppy in one hand and Colette in the other.

'Wahoy!' he said. 'Wahoy, iggly plops!'

Whackleclack

OLD THROG KNELT in the mist, a pointed stone in his hand and a boulder on the ground in front of him.

He had never tried stone-carving before, and it was hard work. Throg had cut himself twice, and some of the letters looked a bit crooked. But that didn't matter: it was the words themselves which counted, not how they were written.

Throg's heart swelled with pride as he thought how

giants for generations to come would look at this boulder and the writing on it:

ISH EZ QUEESH THROG KRAGGLED
O BIMPLESTONK.
(THIS IS WHERE THROG KILLED
THE BEANSTALK.)

They would rejoice and remember the courageous old giant who had saved them from an invasion of iggly plops.

Still swollen with triumphant thoughts, he climbed back over the wall and hobbled along the narrow road which led to the town.

Only when he passed the field where he had dozed the other day did his mind take a different course. He remembered the grinning girl he had seen walking along the same road, and the recollection sparked memories of his own childhood.

Throg's earliest memory was of a toy, a furry animal called Lolshly. The word lolshly meant white, but Throg could only remember his Lolshly being a dirty brownish colour.

Young Throg and his Lolshly had been inseparable: he cuddled the toy in bed and took it everywhere with him. His mother, he remembered, had been less enthusiastic. She said that Lolshly was dirty and smelly and needed a wash. But Throg had refused to hear of such a thing: it was the smell that he *liked*; he would press his nose against Lolshly's body and take deep comforting breaths while he twiddled tufts of grubby fur between finger and thumb.

And then one day Lolshly had disappeared. Throg had fallen asleep in the pram and when he woke up the toy had gone. Vaguely he remembered the search, the tears, the offer of a replacement which he turned down angrily: *nothing* could replace Lolshly. But what he remembered most clearly was his mother telling him that the iggly plops must have taken it.

That was the moment that Throg's hatred for the iggly plops had been born. His search for Lolshly became a search for the tiny wicked thieves who had taken his toy.

He never found a single iggly plop. He told himself

that they must have returned to their own land. But he was in no doubt that they were determined to come back one day – just as determined as he was to stop them.

And now he *had* stopped them! Throg felt another surge of joy and, to match his mood, the sun came out from behind a cloud. It shone brightly and the whole world shone back at it: the raindrops on the grass blades glinted, the buttercups glowed, and even the road seemed to glitter . . . wait a minute, what *was* that bright iggly thing in the middle of the road?

Throg had always prided himself on his excellent eyesight, and even in his old age this was as keen as ever. He bent down to inspect the tiny object in the road.

It was white, and igglier, much igglier, than a jewel in a ring.

It was shiny, and round, and flat, and it had two holes in the middle of it.

It was a whackleclack, the iggliest whackleclack that Throg had ever seen, a whackleclack so iggly that it could only belong to an iggly plop.

The icy lake

'**B**OAT ALL STICKY,' said Poppy.

'It's not a boat, it's a soap dish,' said Stephen.

Colette said nothing. She was feeling seasick. Their soap-dish boat heaved on the bathwater waves, and above them the frightening, grinning face of the boy giant loomed over the side of the bath. He was the one creating the waves, by churning up the bathwater with his hands. The more distressed the children grew the more he grinned.

Now he turned on the cold tap again, and their soapy tub spun round. Colette held on to the edge, feeling giddy, and the giant boy laughed.

'Stop it, you slimy slug!' Stephen shouted. In reply, their tormentor splashed some water over the edge of the soap dish.

'Don't shout at him like that – do you want him to capsize us?' said Colette.

Almost as if he understood her, the boy giant sloshed some more water into their boat.

'All wet,' said Poppy.

The cold water was up to their knees now, that is when they could manage to stand; but the slippery floor and the movement of the boat kept overbalancing them, and they were soon soaked through.

The soap dish was sinking lower and lower in the water.

'Wunk, twunk, thrink . . . GLISHGLURSH!' shouted the boy giant, and an enormous wave crashed over their heads.

Colette gulped a great mouthful before she was swept under the water. It swirled her round and pressed on her from all directions. She hardly knew which way up she was.

No, no, no, she said to herself. *I will not drown in a giant's bath.* Her arms and legs went into action.

Just as she felt she could hold her breath no longer, her head came out of the water.

She spluttered and opened her eyes. There was Stephen, treading water and looking wildly around him. She knew he wouldn't drown. He had been to life-saving classes.

And then she heard Poppy scream.

Her little sister was thrashing about, clinging to the edge of the soap dish as it sank under the water. She couldn't swim.

But now Stephen had reached her and was on his back, his hands under her armpits. 'Keep still, Poppy – don't panic!' he said.

Poppy stopped struggling and allowed Stephen to propel her in circles round the bath. But how long could he keep it up? And how long could Colette carry on treading water like this? The water was like an icy lake. Her arms and legs were beginning to feel quite numb.

Above them came the awful laugh again.

'Heehuckerly iggly plops!'

'It's not *funny*, you scorpion!' spluttered Stephen.

The boy giant reached out for the tap and turned it off.

'At least the current won't be so strong now,' said Colette.

She kept her eye on the giant hand. It moved towards the chain between the two taps . . . the chain which was joined on to the plug.

'Wunk, twunk, thrink . . . HAROOF!' He pulled the chain.

Good, was Colette's first thought. The water level would go down. They wouldn't have to keep swimming for ever.

But then she thought about what happens when a bath empties. She thought about the whirlpool of water being sucked down the plughole at the very end. And she thought about the plughole itself, and the holes in it.

Surely the holes in a giant's plughole wouldn't be big enough for a human being to slip through?

She hardly took in the sound of the front door and

the footsteps on the staircase. But she did hear the voice.

'Zab! Zab!'

It was Jumbeelia.

'Zab! ZAB! Queesh oor oy?' She was just outside the bathroom door.

Suddenly Jumbeelia, their kidnapper, felt like a rescuer. Please come and find us, Jumbeelia. Please! Come in now!

Colette thought it, but Poppy shouted it.

'Big girl! Come here!'

And Jumbeelia did.

The girl giant's voice dropped to a whisper, but it was a furious-sounding whisper.

'Zab! Uth oor *mub* iggly plops! Niffle uth abreg!' she hissed.

The boy giant's voice dropped too. Obviously neither of them wanted their mother to hear.

'Uth oor *mubbin*!' he said.

'Nug! Uth oor *mubbin*!' replied Jumbeelia, pointing to herself before coming out with some more angry sounds.

'I think they're arguing about who owns us,' said Colette.

'*Nobody* owns us!' said Stephen angrily.

Meanwhile the level of the bath was steadily sinking. Colette began to feel herself being pulled towards the plug end. She tried to swim against the current, but only managed to stay in the same place.

Jumbeelia reached into the bath but Zab grabbed her wrist.

Now the girl giant's tone of voice changed: she seemed to be pleading with him, maybe even to be offering something.

'Queesh?' whispered Zab. He sounded interested.

Colette heard Jumbeelia go out, and her heart sank.

The tug of the plughole was becoming stronger. Stephen, still on his back with Poppy in his grip, had been sucked towards it and was swimming in helpless circles around it.

'Come back! Come back, big girl!' Poppy cried.

'Shhhh!' said the boy giant. He leaned over and fished the soap dish out of the water. Roughly, clumsily, he grabbed Stephen and Poppy and put them into it. The next second Colette was beside them. The three of them huddled together on the slippery floor of what had been their boat.

Poppy whimpered and Colette tried to comfort her.

'We'll be all right. At least we're not going to drown,' she said.

They were no longer on the bath sea, but in the air, borne aloft by Zab.

'He's taking us back to Jumbo's room,' muttered Stephen, shivering in his soggy ballet dress as they lurched along.

They peered over the edge of the soap dish and saw Jumbeelia with something in her hand.

'Iggly strimpchogger,' she said.

'It's our lawn mower!' said Stephen indignantly.

Zab was clearly impressed. He put the soap dish down on Jumbeelia's floor and grabbed the lawn mower. They saw him turn the key in the ignition and beam when the engine started up.

'Sweefswoof?' asked Jumbeelia.

'Ootle rootle,' said Zab, and he picked up Poppy.

Stephen was still incensed about the lawn mower. 'They're thieves, all of them!' he said.

'I think they're doing a swap,' said Colette,

remembering how she had once swapped all the toy cars she had collected from cereal packets for the shells Stephen had brought back from a school trip.

Sure enough, Zab handed Poppy over to Jumbeelia.

'Big girl! Nice big girl' cried Poppy. Jumbeelia kissed her and then reached down for Colette and Stephen.

Colette felt ridiculously pleased. Although their escape attempt had failed, anything was better than being at the mercy of Zab.

But Zab was too quick for Jumbeelia. He snatched the soap dish, and Colette and Stephen went whizzing up in it, high above his head.

They heard Jumbeelia protest: 'Niffle uth abreg! Niffle uth abreg!'

Zab laughed his nasty laugh. 'Wunk iggly plop – wunk iggly strimpchogger,' he said.

And though Colette didn't understand the words themselves, she did understand what had happened.

Zab had swapped Poppy for the lawn mower. But he was going to hang on to Colette and Stephen. It was Finders Keepers.

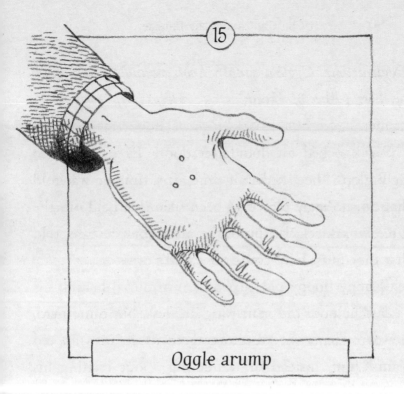

Oggle arump

OLD THROG NO longer spent his days walking round the edgeland. Instead, he walked round the town. In his hand he held the three whackleclacks he had now found.

He had made up a new rhyme. It went like this:

Iggly plops! Iggly plops!   *Little people! Little people!*
Queesh? Queesh? Queesh?   *Where? Where? Where?*

Oggle arump! Oggle arump!   Look around! Look around!
Aheesh! Aheesh! Aheesh!   Help! Help! Help!

Throg knocked on door after door. 'Ev oy oggled o iggly plops?' he asked, but time after time he was told that no, no iggly plop had been seen. He held out the three whackleclacks, but time after time he was told that they must have come off a doll's dress.

'Roopy floopy plop,' people murmured behind his back. The poor old man was harmless, but quite mad. It was a shame he wouldn't agree to go into an old giants' jum, instead of wandering about reciting his strange rhymes.

Today, Throg walked up the front path of a house on the outskirts of town. He had tried this house before but never found anyone in.

He rang at the bell and a woman came to the door.

He asked her the usual question, 'Ev oy oggled o iggly plops?' and received the usual pitying look and the usual answer, 'Nug.'

Throg looked at the woman suspiciously. You couldn't trust anyone. He thought for the thousandth time of the old (but true) bimplestonk story, the one in which the iggly plop had stolen the giant's harp and hen. In that story the giant's wife had hidden the wicked iggly plop from her husband and lied to him. For all he knew, this woman could be lying too.

A girl appeared in the doorway. Throg recognised her – it was the policeman's daughter. She was complaining loudly about how her brother had stolen her collection of conkers, but when she saw Throg she broke off and hid behind her mother's back.

Her mother smiled apologetically, then said 'Yahaw' and closed the door.

Throg stood for a second on the doorstep before setting off on his way. Something was bothering him. Some memory was refusing to come to the surface.

He shrugged and walked back down the path to the road. And then he remembered. This was the same stretch of road where he had found the whackleclacks.

Throg scratched his head and thought. He couldn't quite work it out but it was all very suspicious. He never had trusted the police. He would certainly keep an eye on that house.

16

The battle jar

ZAB'S REMOTE-CONTROLLED car crashed into the bedroom wall.

Stephen managed to slam his hands against the dashboard just in time, but Colette screamed as her head hit the windscreen.

'Are you all right?' Stephen asked.

'I think so. Just another bruise.'

They had been Zab's playthings for a week. It was like being in a torture chamber, and you never knew what the next torture would be. Sometimes he juggled with them. Sometimes he swung them about on his lampshade. Sometimes he dangled them out of the window.

The other day he had put them on a high slippery shelf. 'Glay boff!' he had said, and they realised he wanted to see if they could work out how to get down. He did clap in admiration when Stephen succeeded in sliding down the flex of the alarm clock, but then offered him a red-hot chilli as a reward, forcing him to bite it and then chortling, 'Heehuckerly iggly plop!' when Stephen gasped, his mouth on fire.

Zab didn't always give them such burningly hot food. Usually he threw down some breadcrumbs on to the floor beside a bowl of water. The rim of the bowl came up to their chins and he would laugh as they stood and scooped the water in their cupped hands.

Colette and Stephen were both now permanently dressed in army uniforms from Zab's action figures. The clothes were too big and baggy, but Stephen was hugely relieved that he no longer had to wear the hated pink ballet dress.

It wasn't too bad when Zab played soldiers with them. Usually they were both allowed to be on the winning side, which involved beating up a lot of plastic figures, but once or twice he gave them both swords and tried to make them fight each other.

Back home the pair of them had fought all the time, but now Colette realised that she didn't want to. In fact, they were getting on much better than they ever had done before. Stephen hadn't called her any insect names for days.

Sometimes Jumbeelia tried to get them back. 'Beesh, Zab, beesh! Niffle uth abreg!' they would hear her clamour. But Zab just held them above his head and laughed.

At night they slept in Zab's sock drawer. It was very dark, and the socks didn't smell too clean. Colette found herself missing the doll's-house bedroom.

Even more, she missed her bed at home. She could hardly bear to think of Mum tucking her up or Dad waking her with one of his funny voices, pretending to be the family butler or a Roman slave-driver. But most of all, she missed Poppy. She hated to think how lonely and scared her little sister must be feeling, all on her own in the doll's house.

'We've *got* to get back to Poppy,' she said to Stephen now, sitting in the passenger seat of the crashed car and feeling her forehead for the new bruise.

Just then, Zab grabbed them, one in each hot sweaty hand. He kicked the car, and strode out of the room.

'Maybe he's going to give us back to Jumbeelia?' said Colette hopefully.

'I bet he's going to put us in the bath again,' said Stephen.

They were both wrong. Zab took them somewhere they had never been before – into the garden.

He put them down on the path and then reached into his pocket and placed something beside them. It was their lawn mower.

'I bet Dad's missing that,' said Stephen.

'Don't be stupid! Do you seriously think he's bothering about a lawn mower when all of us are missing?'

'Oh shut up – don't rub it in.'

'Sorry,' said Colette. She blinked back the tears

which were pricking her eyes and looked about her. On one side of the path was a forest of giant grass. Some upside-down plastic flowerpots the size of huts sat on the path beside a desert of a sandpit.

Zab was digging two holes in the sand. He popped Colette and Stephen into the holes and scooped some sand back in around them. They were buried up to their necks.

'It's another of his experiments,' said Stephen gloomily. 'He wants to see if we can get ourselves out.'

The sand was the heavy kind, and they couldn't. Zab laughed and strode away.

'Do you think he's just going to leave us here?' Colette asked in panic. It was terrifying to be abandoned, trapped in the sand, her arms pinioned to her body, unable even to scratch a tickle on her nose.

'No, look – he's coming back.'

Zab squatted on the path beside them. There was something draped over one of his fingers. It was wriggling about like a great pink python.

'Squerple!' he said, dangling it in front of Colette's face.

Colette closed her eyes and turned her head to one side, which was all she could do. She quite liked ordinary worms – in fact, she had once collected them – but this giant one was as thick as her buried arm. It didn't have a proper face, but she could see its mouth quite clearly, opening and closing slightly as if searching for some earth to swallow. 'It's not a snake – it won't bite me,' she told herself She didn't want to give Zab the pleasure of hearing her cry out.

All the same, Zab laughed before tossing the worm away and starting to dig them out.

'Listen,' said Stephen urgently. 'I've thought of a plan. You try and distract him, and I'll hide the lawn mower.'

'What for?'

'Because then when we *do* manage to rescue Poppy and escape, we'll have a getaway car.'

Zab put them down on the path. They exchanged a look, and then Colette started to run.

'Zabbadabbadee! You can't catch me!' she taunted the boy giant.

But Zab didn't seem to want to. He was fiddling about with a jam jar.

'Get his attention! Do a little dance or something!' Stephen egged her on.

Colette hopped about and made faces, but still Zab showed no interest in her. Instead, he lifted Stephen up and put him into the jar.

'Let him out!' Colette cried, suddenly fearful. She ran back up the path.

Stephen was in the circular glass tank, looking white. He wasn't alone. A black-and-yellow stripy creature was crawling up the side of the huge jam jar.

It was a giant wasp, and it was nearly half Stephen's size.

Zab reached in and prodded the wasp with a pin. It buzzed angrily, and Zab handed the pin to Stephen. He took it with a shaking hand.

'Kraggle! Kraggle! Kraggle!' shouted Zab.

The wasp tried to fly out of the jam jar but Zab was too quick for it, and screwed the lid on.

'Don't do that! They need air!' Colette shouted, as if Zab could understand.

Then she watched in horror as the wasp flew round the jar. She could see something sharp sticking out of its tail end. It was the tip of a sting.

Still buzzing, the maddened creature bumped into the side of the jar, and then it bumped into Stephen.

Stephen fell on to his back, dropping the pin and letting out a cry.

Colette stood helplessly outside the glass and saw the wasp land on his face. She knew that the whole sting would be as long and sharp as a dagger. If the wasp pierced him with it he would surely die.

'The pin, Stephen! Get the pin!' she urged him. It was lying on the floor of the jar. Keeping his body as still as he could, Stephen reached out and grabbed it.

The wasp raised its tail end. The sting was poised to plunge into Stephen's chest. He gasped and his eyelids closed.

'Don't give up now!' cried Colette.

Stephen opened his eyes. Gritting his teeth, he lunged out with the pin. The tip of it speared the underside of the wasp and bore the creature into the air above him. As the sting shot out of it, he hurled the pin away from him and scrambled to his feet.

The wasp writhed on the floor of the jar, still skewered by the pin.

Stephen backed away and sat down against the glass wall. He was panting and he looked even whiter than before.

The wasp stopped writhing. It was dead.

Zab clapped. He unscrewed the lid of the jar and seemed about to remove Stephen, but then changed his mind. 'Tweeko!' he cried, and he was off again.

'Stephen, are you all right?' asked Colette, pressing herself against the outside of the jar. She was trembling. How she wished she could climb the steep glass and reach him.

'Yes, but you'll have to see to the lawn mower,' said Stephen faintly. 'Hide it under a flower pot.'

'I don't want to leave you,' she said.

'You must. Think about Poppy. She won't be able to walk all the way to the beanstalk.'

Zab was over by the garden wall. He didn't notice Colette dragging the plastic flower pot towards the lawn mower. It wasn't as heavy as she'd feared. Her hands were still shaking as she lifted a section of the flower pot as high as she could, positioned it over the lawn mower and let it fall.

She was afraid that the clatter would alert Zab, but he had returned to the jam jar and seemed intent on whatever was going on inside it.

Gripped by dread, Colette tiptoed back and saw what Zab found so enthralling.

Stephen and the dead wasp were still in the jar. So was a giant spider. The spider was enormous, and its jointed hairy legs splayed out in all directions, leaving very little space for Stephen, who was holding a new pin.

'Kraggle! Kraggle! Kraggle!' Zab was shouting again.

'He's saying "Kill! Kill! Kill!",' Colette realised, feeling sick. But this time Stephen would not oblige.

Colette could see that the spider wasn't interested in Stephen; it seemed much keener on the dead wasp.

'Kraggle! Flisterflay, iggly plop – *kraggle*!' Zab commanded angrily, but Stephen held the pin behind his back.

'Why should I?' he said. 'It hasn't done anything to me.'

Zab was furious now. He unscrewed the lid of the jam jar and turned it upside down, shaking Stephen, the dead wasp and the live spider out on to the path.

The spider scuttled away. Stephen picked himself up and waved the pin angrily at Zab. 'You're evil!' he shouted.

Zab lifted a foot to stamp on Stephen.

'Stop!' shouted Colette, grabbing Zab's undone shoelace.

Zab wobbled, missed Stephen and kicked Colette instead. She fell to the ground.

'Leave my sister alone!' Stephen climbed on to Zab's trainer and dug the pin into his ankle.

'Askorp! Askorp, oy frikely plop!' Zab yelped with pain as Stephen jumped off his trainer and ran down the path.

Colette picked herself up and watched Zab catch up with Stephen and step over him. Stephen dodged sideways, and ran towards an enormous wooden building. 'It must be the giants' garden shed,' thought Colette.

The floor of the building was propped up by bricks. She saw Stephen run under it.

'Pecky iggly plop!' shouted Zab. He found a stick and started poking it under the shed.

'Come on, Colette!' shouted Stephen. 'It's safe under here!'

Colette ran down the path towards the shed. But Zab spotted her. He snatched her up. Then he looked around. Colette guessed he was looking for the lawn mower.

'Queesh ez o strimpchogger?' he said, and squeezed her angrily. It hurt.

'Zab!' came a voice from the house. It was the giant mother, calling him.

Without letting go of Colette, Zab poked the stick under the shed one last time. Colette kicked and struggled, desperate to escape his grip, but it only tightened. Then, in his nastiest voice, Zab shouted at Stephen:

'Ootle rootle, iggly plop! Yahaw!'

He turned on his heel and strode towards the house, with Colette still in his hand.

17

Sweefswoof

Z AB STOMPED UP the stairs, clutching the girl iggly plop. He was angry with her, almost as angry as he was with the boy iggly plop. It would serve him right to be left out in the garden. Zab hoped that an owl or a fox would get him.

As for the girl, she was turning out to be pretty useless. She was a rotten fighter, and she had a cunning streak too: Zab was convinced that she had hidden the precious strimpchogger that he had sweefswoofed with

Jumbeelia for the iggliest plop. Now he wouldn't be able to take it on holiday with him.

Zab wasn't specially looking forward to staying with his grandfather. There wasn't much to do there, and it would have been fun to have the strimpchogger to play with. Still, he thought, at least he would get more sweets, chocolates and crisps at Grishpij's house than he did at home. And at least Jumbeelia wouldn't be there. Also, Grishpij had a dog. It was a silly yappy thing, but to the iggly plop it would be bigger than an elephant. She would probably be terrified – especially now that the nasty iggly boy was no longer around to protect her.

Zab smiled at this thought. This miniature girl was the perfect victim for the experiments and tortures which he could only dream of inflicting on his life-size sister. He squeezed her more tightly as he carried her into his room. Still smiling, he zipped her up in his sponge bag, which he then put into his hold-all. Her muffled squawks and protests stopped when Mij came into the room. Zab had noticed before that the iggly plops seemed to be nervous of his mother.

He was glad to see Mij because he had been

wondering how many poddums spending money she would be giving him.

'Heek munchly poddums?' he asked.

'Thrink,' she replied.

Only thrink poddums! That was hardly anything!

Zab grumbled, then yelled, then threatened not to go away at all, but Mij refused to increase the amount. She told him to get washed, comb his hair and bring his hold-all downstairs.

Well, thought Zab, when she had gone, if she wouldn't help him he would have to help himself. He knew that Jumbeelia often left money lying around. He slunk into her room.

To his annoyance, she was in there, sitting on the floor with her back turned to him. She hadn't heard him come in, so he crept up on her and pulled her hair.

'Ow!' she yelled. 'Glay awook, Zab!'

But Zab didn't go away. He was too interested in what Jumbeelia was doing.

She was posting coins – a lot of coins – into a money box he had never seen before. It was bright red, and the slot looked as if it were designed to receive iggly letters rather than coins; in fact, the whole thing looked just like an iggly pobo. It was a wonderful money box, and Zab knew that he had to have it.

He made a grab but he wasn't fast enough. Jumbeelia, who had just posted the last coin into the slot, jumped up and ran towards the door, the iggly pobo in her hand. Zab heard the coins rattle inside it. It sounded almost full.

'Askorp!' he called. Jumbeelia stopped in the doorway but looked ready to take off again.

Zab eyed the beely red object and thought about all the coins inside it. He thought about his measly amount of spending money. Then he thought about the girl iggly plop inside his sponge bag.

'Sweefswoof?' he suggested.

The running-away collection

ONE MOMENT COLETTE was nearly suffocating inside Zab's dank, smelly sponge bag; the next moment she was back in Jumbeelia's room, inside the doll's house. She was relieved, but too confused and troubled to feel really happy.

Jumbeelia had gone out of the room, closing the door behind her. There was no sign of Poppy.

'Poppy? Poppy, where are you?'

The sitting room and the kitchen were empty.

Colette climbed the stairs and found Poppy on her sardine-tin bed. She wasn't asleep – her eyes were open – but she was lying perfectly still, staring at the ceiling.

'Poppy, it's me. Are you all right?'

Poppy came out of her trance then. She jumped off the bed and hugged Colette.

'Back 'gain! Back 'gain,' she kept saying. Then she ran to the window and said, 'Stephen coming?'

'No. Not yet, anyway. He's in the garden. Zab left him there.'

Poppy started to cry.

Colette put an arm round her. 'He'll be all right,' she said. 'He'll come and find us. Or we'll go and find him. We'll all be together again soon.'

She wished she believed her own words. She thought of the wasp and the spider, and tried not to think about any other giant-size creatures that Stephen might meet out in the garden. How would he keep warm at night? What would he eat and drink?

Colette was too worried to feel hungry herself, and when Jumbeelia came back with two giant spaghetti hoops she left most of hers.

'Have nice sweety,' suggested Poppy, pointing to a giant button strewn with huge sugar grains, but Colette couldn't be tempted.

With a slight sigh, Jumbeelia held an enormous cornflake up to Colette's lips. Colette tried to nibble at it but just felt sick.

Impatiently, the girl giant put the cornflake down beside the sugar grains and went out of the room, once again closing the door.

'At least we won't have to play farms,' said Colette. Then, eyeing the leftovers on the table, 'We should keep these, you know. Let's hide them in the fridge.'

They broke up the cornflake into little pieces and put them in one of the doll's saucepans, along with the sugar grains.

'Leck-shun!' said Poppy. It was her longest word, and she looked triumphant.

'Yes, a collection. A running-away collection,' said Colette.

'Run away, find Stephen.'

'We can't yet. Jumbeelia's being very careful about

keeping her door closed. But one of these days she'll forget. So let's look for some other things for the running-away collection. Not just food – maybe some blankets too . . . and weapons.'

Jumbeelia's bedroom was already in a mess again, with stuff strewn all over the floor. Colette began to feel a little more cheerful as they hunted for things they thought might be useful. In spite of everything, it was good to be collecting again.

'Look, Poppy – we can wrap food up in these sweet papers. And these giant badges could be good as shields.'

'Nice hats,' said Poppy. She had come across the acorn cups again.

'They might come in handy,' said Colette, though she couldn't quite think how.

Then, 'Peggy line!' Poppy called out, pointing to the washing line, complete with pegged-out sheets, towels and clothes, that Jumbeelia had snatched along with them.

'Brilliant, Poppy. And look! She's pegged our old clothes on it. Stephen will be dead pleased to get his jeans and T-shirt back!'

Poppy was entranced when they came upon a box of

Christmas-tree decorations: gleaming silver balls, sparkly angels and paper lanterns all as big as themselves. She fell in love with a feathery Christmas-tree robin.

'Big bird run away too,' she said.

'Big bird won't be any use to us,' said Colette, and Poppy's face fell. 'But these would. Aren't they pretty?' Colette held up two drawstring bags made of gold glittery material, with ribbon handles. 'The giants probably put sweets in them at Christmas time, and hang them on the tree.'

'Sweety for Poppy,' said Poppy hopefully.

'No. But we can put the stuff we've collected in them and carry everything on our backs when we escape.'

It was beginning to get dark and Colette suddenly felt exhausted. Poppy yawned too and said, 'Bed time. Big girl tuck up Poppy.'

But Jumbeelia still hadn't come back so it was Colette who tucked up her sister and sang her a lullaby. She fell asleep quickly.

Colette couldn't get to sleep. She was too worried about Stephen. She was still awake when Jumbeelia went to bed. Listening again to the giant mother telling a bedtime story, she wished she could understand their language.

Jumbeelia didn't seem to be paying much attention to the story; she kept interrupting, and Colette heard her say the word 'spratchkin' over and over again.

Later still, when the light was out and Jumbeelia was snoring softly, Colette heard a hooting noise from outside. It sounded horribly like an owl. She remembered how bravely Stephen had fought the wasp and refused to fight the spider. She remembered him shouting, 'Leave my sister alone!' and jabbing Zab's ankle with the pin, and she realised that she was missing him every bit as much as she missed Mum and Dad. In fact, it seemed funny that she often used to think she hated Stephen. If they could all be together again, she felt that she wouldn't mind being called all the insect names in the world.

There was the owl again. Colette tried not to imagine how big a giant owl would be, or how sharp its claws or beak would feel.

But what was this new noise? It sounded like an

engine being started, somewhere a long way below her, out in the garden. There it was again: some revving noises, this time followed by a long dull roar.

Colette felt a bubble of hope swelling inside her. It was the lawn mower! Stephen must have found it under the flowerpot. Everything was going to work out. She drifted off to sleep.

She woke with a start in the middle of the night.

Someone or something was tapping at the window.

Though it was still dark she could just make out the dim square of the doll's-house window. It had no curtains. There didn't seem to be anyone outside it, and the tapping had stopped now.

Colette sat up in bed. She listened. All was silent.

But she *had* heard a tapping, she was sure.

She cast her eyes round the room. They were growing used to the darkness, and she could make out the shapes of Stephen's empty bed and Poppy's sardine tin.

Then she looked back at the window and her heart missed a beat.

A glinting green eye was staring in at her.

Spratchkin

'OGGLE, GRISHMIJ, OGGLE!'

Jumbeelia laughed, pointed, and tugged at her grandmother's sleeve.

Obediently, Grishmij watched the spratchkin chasing a leaf. She smiled faintly and then went back to the iggly yellow sock she was knitting for the bobbaleely.

Jumbeelia picked the spratchkin up, hoping it would stay in her arms, but it wasn't in a woozly mood;

it jumped down and was off after the leaf again, batting it down the path and under the garden shed.

Jumbeelia laughed again. She hadn't felt as happy as this for ages. It was a lovely sunny day. Zab was still away at Grishpij's house, she had Grishmij all to herself, she was soon to have a new brother or sister, and – best of all – she had the beely beely spratchkin. Oh, and the iggly plops too, of course; she had almost forgotten about them.

The spratchkin was still crouched by the garden shed, and every now and then would shoot a black paw underneath it. Was it trying to get the leaf back, or had it discovered something even more interesting under there?

Jumbeelia was about to go and look, when she heard a familiar voice.

Iggly plops! Iggly plops!
Queesh? Queesh? Queesh?
Oggle arump! Oggle arump!
Aheesh! Aheesh! Aheesh!

It was old Throg on his rounds again. There he was, leaning over the gate and beckoning to Grishmij, who put down her knitting and went to ask what he wanted.

It was the same old question: 'Ev oy oggled o iggly plops?'

Grishmij smiled and shook her head. 'Nug – yimp.' She hadn't seen the iggly plops, and she didn't believe in them, though she was too kind to tell old Throg that.

Jumbeelia smiled too. She imagined what Grishmij would say if she found out that Throg *wasn't* mad to believe in the iggly plops; that two iggly plops were in her bedroom at this very moment.

If only she could talk to Throg! She would love to put him right about the iggly plops, to tell him that they weren't the dangerous creatures he thought they were. But she still felt shy of him, and she certainly didn't want to give away the hiding place of her two pet iggly plops.

She was sure that Throg would never discover those two, but she did worry that he might find the boy that Zab had lost. She still felt very cross with Zab about that. Fancy bringing them down into the garden!

Thinking about the iggly plops, Jumbeelia remembered guiltily that she had forgotten to give them any lunch. She hadn't played with them much the last few days, either; she'd been too busy playing outside with the spratchkin.

In any case, the iggly plops weren't quite as much fun as they used to be. The wild one wasn't getting any tamer, and even the iggliest one was a bit droopy these days. Maybe they were missing the boy. Maybe Jumbeelia ought to go back down the bimplestonk and look for another one to replace him. That should cheer them up. And maybe – wonderful thought! – she might even find some iggly spratchkins down there.

Old Throg gave them both a last suspicious look and was on his way.

Grishmij went back to her knitting. The spratchkin seemed to have forgotten about whatever was under the garden shed and was patting at a snail.

Jumbeelia picked up the snail. Studying it, she wondered if all snails had exactly the same squirls on their shells or if each one was different . . .

The monster on the bed

'I HUNGRY,' SAID Poppy.

Colette noticed that she was beginning to talk in a more grown-up way. Only a few days ago she would have said 'Poppy hungry'.

Jumbeelia had forgotten to give them any lunch again.

'We'll have to eat something from the running-away collection,' said Colette. But there were only a few giant sugar grains left: the two hungry children had eaten all the cornflakes and raisins.

Colette was trying to decide whether to give in to Poppy's demands for 'more sweeties' when they heard Jumbeelia come into the room.

'I expect she'll feed us now,' said Colette.

But the girl giant's footsteps thudded towards a different part of the room.

Poppy's face fell. 'I still hungry,' she said miserably.

'It's no use telling *me* that,' snapped Colette. Then she saw that Poppy was nearly crying. 'Come on,' she said, more gently. 'Let's go and show Jumbeelia how hungry we are. Practise clutching your tummy.'

They found their way to where Jumbeelia was lying on the floor by a sheet of polythene.

'Big girl got snails like 'Lette,' said Poppy.

And so she had. At one end of the polythene sheet were some giant leaves and blades of grass, and at the other end were three gigantic coiled shells.

'Wunk, twunk, thrink, GLAY!' shouted Jumbeelia.

A rubbery head protruded from one of the shells, and two transparent horns with eyes at the end of them quivered. The giant snail slithered a few inches along the polythene. Jumbeelia clapped her hands.

'I think it's supposed to be a race,' said Colette.

Jumbeelia noticed them then. 'Wahoy, iggly plops,' she said.

'*Now*, Poppy!' ordered Colette.

She and Poppy clutched their tummies and made what they hoped were hungry faces.

Jumbeelia laughed. 'Heehuckerly iggly plops!' she said. Then she turned back to the snails.

'I know!' said Colette. 'Let's pretend to eat the grass. That should give her the idea.'

They grabbed two blades of the giant grass and began to nibble.

Jumbeelia did take more notice then. 'Loopy iggly plops! Glay jum,' she said. She picked them up, one in each hand, and took them back to the doll's house.

'Dinner coming now!' said Poppy. And it was – but not the sort of dinner they wanted. Instead, Jumbeelia pushed a bundle of grass in through the doll's-house door.

'Beely strimp!' she said, and went back to the snails.

'Oh no!' said Colette. 'Now she thinks we really *like* grass.'

She tried not to cry – she wanted to be as brave for Poppy as Stephen had been for her – but she couldn't help it. She was hungry and she was missing Stephen, but what made the tears come so fast was the feeling that Jumbeelia didn't seem to care about them any more. Compared with Zab, Jumbeelia had been almost like a friend: she was a fellow collector, and such a kind and gentle one, or so it had seemed. Why had she let them down like this?

'Cheer up, 'Lette,' said Poppy, stroking her leg. This just made Colette burst out into louder sobs.

'Jumbeelia's so *heartless*!'

But as she said the words she knew in a flash that they weren't true, that Jumbeelia didn't really mean to be cruel or unkind. 'No, she's not heartless – she's just like me.'

Colette remembered how her mother always accused her of losing interest in her collections. In just the same way, Jumbeelia was losing interest in them. But as she forgave the girl giant, Colette found herself feeling worse instead of better. Supposing Jumbeelia forgot to feed them ever again? What hope was there for them?

Poppy interrupted her thoughts. 'I thirsty,' she said.

Colette stopped crying then, not because she felt better, but because she suddenly felt cold all over.

She knew that people could go without food for days, weeks even. But if you don't have anything to drink, you die.

'Go in garden, find Stephen, get puddle water,' said Poppy.

If only it was that simple! Even though Jumbeelia didn't often play with them now, she was still careful to keep her door closed, especially at night, when the monster kitten slept on her bed.

Thinking about the kitten gave Colette an idea. Jumbeelia always put down a saucer of milk for it when she went to bed.

'We can't get into the garden yet, but I *will* get us a drink. I'll get it tonight,' she promised Poppy.

That night a full moon shone through the gap in Jumbeelia's curtains. The girl giant was asleep, and the kitten purred on her bed.

In the doll's house, Colette whispered to Poppy:

'Keep very still while I tie this end of the cotton round your wrist.'

The thread of cotton led out of the doll's-house window and across the piles of clutter on Jumbeelia's floor. The other end of it was tied around the feathery robin from the Christmas-tree collection, who now sat in a nest made of tinsel and scraps of paperchain. These would make a good rustle if the thread was pulled.

'Now, remember, Poppy,' said Colette. 'you must keep very still – stiller than you've ever been in your life, probably – but *don't* go to sleep whatever you do. And remember what to do if I call you.'

'Pull string,' said Poppy.

Slowly and carefully Colette opened the front door of the doll's house.

She stood for a minute or so in the doorway. Pinned to her front and back were two of the giant badges. In her hand was a saucepan from the doll's-house kitchen.

Colette listened. The kitten's purr was still loud and strong. Jumbeelia wasn't snoring but Colette was pretty sure from the sound of her deep regular breathing that she was fast asleep.

'You can do it,' she told herself.

Jumbeelia's floor was more of an obstacle course than ever. Colette had to go slowly and be careful not to bump into anything. By the moonlight she could just about make out the different objects.

She came to the plastic cows that she had tried to milk on the first day. They looked quite real in the dim light, and Colette wished they wouldn't stare at her like that.

Just then her foot caught in something. She stumbled and fell.

The kitten stopped purring. Colette kept very still, and it started up again. She counted silently to a hundred, uncoiled the lace from one of Jumbeelia's trainers which had tripped her up, and set off once more.

The purring sounded much louder now. She was getting nearer to Jumbeelia's bed. She rounded a mountain of giant egg boxes. Beyond them she could see the white saucer of milk.

She crossed the last stretch of mossy carpet.

Would there be any milk left in the saucer?

'Please let there be some – please!' she prayed.

She peered down into the white saucer and saw whiteness. Was it just the bottom of the saucer? In the dim light she couldn't tell. She blew gently and the white surface dimpled and rippled – it was milk!

She leaned over and dipped the saucepan into it. Tilting it carefully she filled it almost to the brim.

The full saucepan was heavy and she had to concentrate on keeping her balance as she lifted it out again.

Greedily she gulped some of the milk. Then she stood still, listening to the kitten's purring and to the thumping of her own heart.

Holding the saucepan steadily, she began the return journey.

She rounded the egg boxes and followed the same route back until she saw the cows.

That's where I tripped over the shoelace, she remembered. I'd better go a different way.

She edged round some giant dominoes and came to a pile of grass and leaves – more food for the snails, she supposed.

Was it her imagination, or was one of the leaves

moving slightly? Colette stood still and stared at it.

From behind the leaf a face appeared – a slimy greenish face with two probing glistening horns.

Colette gasped and took a step backwards, then told herself firmly, 'It's only a big snail – it can't hurt me.' She leant against an upright domino and took a few deep breaths.

The domino collapsed.

Colette staggered and managed not to fall. But what was this terrible noise? This series of deafening clacks that sounded like a wooden house collapsing?

Frozen with fear, Colette realized she had toppled a line of dominoes.

'Stay asleep!' she begged the kitten.

But it didn't. It woke up and sprang off the bed.

'Poppy, *pull*!'

Nothing happened.

She's gone to sleep, thought Colette.

And then, from the Christmas-tree collection came the rustling of the robin in its tinsel and paperchain nest. Poppy had pulled the thread!

The kitten sped towards the new noise. Colette

heard it pounce, and the rustling grew louder as it tussled with the feathery decoration.

She hardly dared to move, yet she knew she must before the kitten got bored with the robin.

Still carrying the precious milk, she set off once more towards the doll's house. She could see it now, and could even make out the cotton, which was jerking about in a tug of war, with Poppy tweaking one end and the kitten mauling the robin at the other end.

Then it snapped.

'All fall down,' came a voice from the doll's house.

Colette had nearly reached the front door. The rustling of tinsel, feathers and paper grew less frantic and then stopped altogether.

Ten more steps, Colette thought, willing herself to take them.

She didn't hear the kitten run towards her, but she felt the heavy blow as its paw hit the shield on her back. She fell forwards.

'Naughty cat stop!' Poppy ran out of the doll's house.

'No, Poppy! Go back!' yelled Colette.

But she was too late. The kitten pounced on Poppy.

It knocked her over. Poppy screamed as the black furry monster picked her up in its mouth.

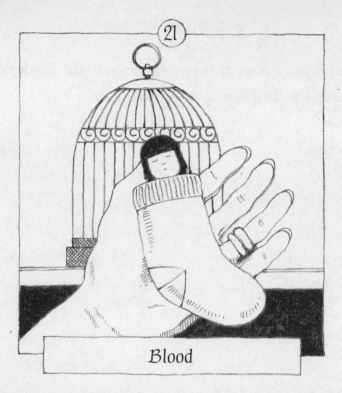

Blood

GRISHMIJ WAS WOKEN by a scream and a shout of 'Nug nug NUG!' Was Jumbeelia having a nightmare?

Within seconds Grishmij was out of bed and on the landing. She opened Jumbeelia's bedroom door, and the spratchkin streaked out.

'Pecky, *pecky* spratchkin!' yelled Jumbeelia. She was kneeling on the floor, cradling something in her hand, and tears were streaming down her cheeks.

Grishmij knelt down too, and put an arm round her. Jumbeelia had placed one hand on top of the other, hiding whatever it was she was holding.

Grishmij stroked Jumbeelia's hair and asked her what the matter was. At first her granddaughter just sobbed, but at last the words came.

'Grishmij! Grishmij! O spratchkin kraggled o iggly plop!'

Then Grishmij noticed the blood stain on the carpet. And as she looked at it, a fresh drop dripped from Jumbeelia's hands – and another and another.

Jumbeelia looked down at the blood too, and then up at her grandmother through her tears.

'Grishmij! Grishmij!' she cried, and she lifted the hand that was hiding her secret.

In Jumbeelia's other palm lay a tiny white doll. It was dressed in a lacy nighty and a stripy football jumper.

'Iggly plop! Iggly plop!' Jumbeelia sobbed, as if the doll was real.

Grishmij was more concerned about the blood than the doll. How had Jumbeelia hurt herself? Had the spratchkin scratched her?

Jumbeelia shook her head. 'Iggly plop,' she kept repeating, and then, again, 'O spratchkin kraggled o iggly plop.'

She held the doll out to her grandmother. 'Oggle!' she said. Grishmij took a closer look at it, and noticed something extraordinary. The blood was dripping out of the doll's arm.

It wasn't a doll. It really was an iggly plop. And what's more, it wasn't dead. It lay quite still but Grishmij saw it blink.

Very gently, Grishmij took the creature from Jumbeelia's hand. She peeled off the football jumper. One sleeve came off easily but the blood from the wound caused the other sleeve to stick to the iggly plop's arm. Grishmij continued to pull it, and with a little jerk it came away.

'Ow!' said the iggly plop.

Jumbeelia gasped. 'Nug kraggled!' she whispered.

Grishmij knew just what to do next. They took the iggly plop into the bathroom and Grishmij washed its arm. The wound was long but not as deep as she had feared. Jumbeelia fetched a handkerchief, and Grishmij cut a strip off it which she made into a bandage.

The iggly plop was still quite floppy as Grishmij wound the bandage round and round its arm. Although it seemed to be aware of what was happening, it was obviously still suffering from shock.

Grishmij knew that birds and small animals could die of shock and she wondered if this creature would still be alive in the morning. Well, they could only do their best.

While Jumbeelia nursed the iggly plop, Grishmij fetched the old birdcage from the attic. It had sat there ever since Zab had let his canary escape. She gave it a good dust and put some cotton wool inside it.

The kitchen was the warmest room in the house, so they put the cage on the dresser. They filled the food and water containers with cornflakes and orange juice, which Jumbeelia seemed sure the iggly plop would like. Grishmij wondered how she knew this, but decided to save any questions for the morning.

They put the creature inside one of the socks which Grishmij had knitted for the bobbaleely, laying it gently down on the cotton wool and covering it with a pile of handkerchiefs.

Only then did Jumbeelia clap her hand to her mouth and say, 'O ithry iggly plop!'

Another one? Surely not? But Jumbeelia insisted that there *was* another one in her bedroom. They must find it and put it in the cage, to save it from the spratchkin.

After a quick and unsuccessful search of the messy bedroom, Jumbeelia agreed to go to bed, but only if they first shut the spratchkin in Zab's bedroom.

In fact it was already in there, batting a plastic war figure about the floor. There was no sign of any bones or blood, so Grishmij managed to reassure Jumbeelia that it couldn't have eaten the second iggly plop – if indeed it did exist.

She tucked her granddaughter up and went back to her own room.

She was just dropping off to sleep when she was woken again, this time by the ringing of the frangle on her bedside table. It was Jumbeelia's father phoning from the hospital with the news they had all been waiting for.

Grishmij didn't wake Jumbeelia again, but she looked forward to telling her in the morning that she had a new iggly sister.

Alone

COLETTE SAT ON the dark stair and shivered. Beside her lay the plastic railway line and her glittery running-away bag. The ribbon had been cutting into her shoulders, so she had taken the bag off for a quick rest. Not that it felt like a proper rest; Colette's mind was too troubled for that.

Sitting there, she realised that this was the very same stair on which Zab had discovered them all – only about two weeks ago, though it seemed like a lifetime.

That was a dreadful moment, but at least they were all together then.

She had never felt so lonely in her life. Up to now there had always been Stephen or Poppy, and now there was no one.

Missing Stephen was an ache which Colette had grown used to, but missing Poppy was a sharp new pain. She could hardly bear to think about her little sister, and yet she could think of nothing else. Where was she? And was she alive or dead?

Colette realised how much Poppy had changed since their capture: she was no longer just a little pest; she had become a real friend. She had played her part in the milk raid so well, keeping still and then pulling the thread at just the right time to distract the kitten. She had done everything perfectly – right up until the last minute when, with her old fearlessness, she had rushed out of the doll's house to try to save her big sister.

'And now I'm going to save *you*, Poppy.' Colette heaved the running-away bag on to her back and positioned the railway line once more.

The house was quiet. Colette knew that Jumbeelia

and the old lady had gone back to their bedrooms and that the monster kitten was safely shut away in Zab's room; she had seen all this from the landing, where she had hidden earlier.

'But please, no more phone calls!' she said to herself. That sudden ringing, as loud as a fire alarm, had startled her so much that she had nearly fallen off her railway-line slide.

Poppy was downstairs somewhere, and that thought kept Colette going, step by step – slide, bump; slide, bump – right to the bottom of the giant staircase.

Which way now? When Zab had taken her and Stephen out into the garden he had turned left and carried them through a kitchen. That was as good a place as any to start looking for Poppy.

It was lighter down here; a lamp in the hall had been left on. In the distance Colette could see that the kitchen door was ajar, and she made her way towards it.

She was stopped in her tracks by a noise upstairs. The kitten was scratching at Zab's bedroom door, trying to get out.

But it can't get out, she told herself. It can't. It won't.

All the same, she started to run, the heavy bag bumping against the badge-shield on her back.

And now she was in the dark kitchen.

'Poppy!' she whispered.

She said it a little louder, but still there was no reply.

The distant scratching seemed to have stopped. The only sound was a low hum coming from the giant fridge.

As her eyes grew used to the darkness, Colette saw that there was a gap between the fridge and the cupboard beside it. She slid into it. The hum was horribly loud now, but at least this felt like quite a safe hiding place. She turned to have a better look at the room she was in.

A table and chairs. Cupboards. A stack of vegetable baskets beside a towering dresser. As she gazed up at the dresser, the moon came out from behind a cloud and shone through the kitchen window, and Colette saw the cage.

What was in it? A bird? A mouse? A hamster, perhaps?

It couldn't be Poppy, could it?

'Poppy! Poppy, are you there?' Colette said it as loudly as she dared.

Silence.

'Poppy! Poppy, are you all right?'

Still there was no sound from the cage. But there *was* a sound of loud footsteps outside the house.

A key turned in the back door. A sudden bright light flooded the room and Colette edged her way to the very back of the fridge and then behind it.

The fridge's hum sounded louder than ever; and there was a different kind of humming too. Whoever had come into the kitchen was humming a cheerful tune. The voice was low – much lower than Zab's voice. Could it be the giant father?

The humming stopped suddenly, in the middle of the tune.

'Wahoy!' Colette heard the giant man murmur. She heard his footsteps, followed by a softer, metallic sound. He must be opening the door of the cage.

Then she heard him gasp and exclaim, 'Iggly plop!'

Beely bobbaleely

J UMBEELIA'S FATHER, PIJ, was scraping a carrot at the
kitchen table.

The spratchkin jumped up and tried to bat it out of
his hand.

'Pecky, pecky, pecky!' he said with a chuckle. He put
down the knife and tickled the spratchkin under the
chin. Then he pushed her gently off the table. He was
in a good mood. As he began to cut the carrot into thin
strips, he burst into song:

Beely beely bobbaleely,

Bobbaleely mubbin,

Oy whedderwhay woor jum, woor chay

Fa sprubbin, sprubbin, sprubbin!

(Lovely lovely baby,

Baby mine,

You fill our home, our land

With joy, joy, joy!)

It was an old song, and he had never particularly cared about the words before, but now they seemed full of truth and meaning. The new bobbaleely *was* beely. At five days old, she was absolutely beautiful, from the black hair on her pink head to her ten perfect iggly toenails. And tomorrow she would be coming home!

Pij got up and poked one of the carrot strips between the bars of the cage on the dresser. 'Iggly plop! Iggly plop!' he called softly.

Usually Jumbeelia or Grishmij fed the iggly plop, but this afternoon they were both at the hospital, visiting Mij and the new bobbaleely.

'Beely frimmot!' said Pij, waggling the carrot strip about in an attempt to coax the iggly plop from her nest.

Here she came at last. A sudden dart, and she had

snatched the frimmot from his hand.

She wasn't much more than a bobbaleely herself, Pij realised. He was surprised at how protective he felt; maybe it was because he had first seen her the same night that his own bobbaleely was born. If only she wasn't so timid! If she was this scared of him, how was she going to feel about Zab when he came home from Grishpij's house tomorrow?

Pij had been hoping she would learn to say thank you. 'Oidle oy! Oidle oy!' he prompted her now, willing her to parrot the words back to him. Five days in the cage, and the iggly plop hadn't spoken a single word of Groilish, though he, Grishmij and Jumbeelia had all been trying to teach her. Jumbeelia said that the creature *could* speak a different, nonsense language, but Pij had never heard her.

'Oidle oy! Oidle oy!' he repeated, but the iggly plop just backed away into her cotton-wool nest and nibbled at the strip of frimmot.

No one had yet dared to tell Mij about the new pet. Pij feared that she might hand the creature over to old Throg, or else dump her on the compost heap in the garden, which is what she told him she had done with the iggly blebber.

If the iggly plop could learn to say just a few words of Groilish, maybe she would win Mij's heart.

'Wahoy! Wahoy, iggly plop!' Pij tried again, but the only result was a chirrup and a soft thud from the sratchkin. It had leapt up on to the dresser and was staring intently at the cage.

The iggly plop trembled, cowered, and then burrowed under a handkerchief. Although her wound was healing well, her terror of the sratchkin was as great as ever.

Pij pushed the sratchkin on to the floor again, remembering the job he had been planning to do. He poked the remaining strips of frimmot into the cage, then fetched a saw and set to work on the back door. He was cutting out a square of wood from the bottom of the door, so that he could fit a flap for the sratchkin.

The sratchkin watched him briefly, but then padded to her favourite place, which was beside the fridge. She shot a paw down one side of it. A dusty pea rolled out. Instead of playing with it, the sratchkin continued to crouch, wriggle her haunches and stare at the dark gap. Pij wondered if she had seen a mouse, but he was too happy sawing away to bother to investigate.

As he sawed, he struck up the song again:

Beely beely bobbaleely,
Bobbaleely mubbin,
Oy whedderwhay oor jum, oor chay
Fa . . .

He paused to push at the square of wood, which clattered to the floor. At the same time an iggly voice from the cage completed the last three words of the song:

'Sprubbin! Sprubbin! Sprubbin!'

The bridge of doom

A T LAST THERE was a way out!

And at last it was safe to tell Poppy. The kitchen was dark and the house was quiet. All the giants must be in bed.

Colette stepped out from her hiding place. It was always a relief to get away from the deafening hum of the fridge. She had spent five days behind it, with only Poppy's leftovers and anything else she could scavenge during the night to eat.

'Poppy! Poppy, are you awake?'

'Yes. I got carrots,' said Poppy proudly. 'One, two, three, throw.'

A piece of giant carrot as long as Colette's arm landed on the floor.

'Good shot, Poppy,' said Colette. (Poppy's leftovers often landed, uselessly, on the surface of the dresser.) 'But I won't eat it now. We can take it with us.'

'Take it in the garden, see Stephen?' asked Poppy.

'Yes,' said Colette, trying not to sound doubtful. She didn't really know if Stephen *was* still in the garden – she hadn't heard the lawn mower for days – but there was no point in worrying Poppy. Instead, Colette told her, 'There's a cat-flap. We can escape!'

'No,' said Poppy. 'Naughty cat might get us.'

'We'll be fine,' said Colette, as confidently as she could. 'It won't get us. It's upstairs, I'm sure.'

Poppy didn't answer straight away. Then she said, 'All right,' very quietly.

Colette was scared of the giant kitten too, but her main fear was a different one. Before they could escape she would have to climb up and rescue Poppy from her cage, and she didn't know if she had the strength to do it. Inside her cage, Poppy had been fed and pampered by the giants. Her arm had nearly healed and she had put on weight. But as Poppy had grown stronger, Colette, living on a diet of scraps and leftovers, had become weaker.

A worse problem than hunger was thirst. If it wasn't for the juicy tomato which had rolled out of a shopping bag, unspotted by the giants, Colette thought she might have died. She had hidden the tomato behind the fridge and had been nibbling and sucking away at it for the last few days.

Peering up through the gloom at the cage on the dresser, she suddenly felt dizzy. And I haven't even started climbing yet, she thought.

Beside the dresser stood the tall stack of plastic vegetable baskets. They reminded Colette of something. What was it?

Then it came to her. 'The Death Tower,' she said out loud.

That was Stephen's name for one of the climbing frames in an adventure playground back home. The

Death Tower was taller than a house and had five platforms. To reach the top one you had to walk along a scary sloping bridge which Stephen called the Bridge of Doom.

Stephen absolutely loved that sort of thing, but Colette had only climbed the Death Tower once, to prove to him that she wasn't the 'cowardly cockroach' he kept calling her. She could still feel the wave of dizzy panic that had hit her when she'd made the mistake of looking down from the Bridge of Doom.

If only Stephen were here now! But it was no use thinking that.

'I'm coming, Poppy,' she said, and set out across the kitchen floor, dragging the length of yellow plastic behind her. It had been a railway line and a slide, and now it was going to be a bridge.

The vegetable baskets were high at the back and sides but low at the front. It was easy enough to heave herself into the bottom one, which was full of giant potatoes.

Colette clambered up the round dirty boulders to the top of the potato hill. She reached up to dump the railway line into the basket above. Then, gripping the front rim of the basket, she managed to swing herself up into it.

Onions this time. It was harder to climb them because their papery skins kept flaking off. As her fingernails scrabbled at the flesh beneath the skins her eyes began to sting from the onion juice, and soon they were streaming with painful tears. Still, she struggled to the top and heaved herself up to the next basket.

'Nearly there now?' came Poppy's voice, as if Colette was on a car journey.

'Yes, nearly there,' said Colette, though there were still two more baskets to go. As it turned out, these were full of parsnips and carrots, which were quite knobbly and so easier to climb than the round potatoes and onions.

Now came the really tricky part. The rim of the top basket was very nearly as high as the surface of the dresser, but there was a gap between them.

'This is where you come in,' she said to the railway line. It felt like a kind of friend now. After all, it had got her all the way down the giant stairs. But it was one thing sliding down a carpeted staircase, step by step, and quite another to cross a narrow bridge with no railing – especially in the darkness, when the bridge sloped and the drop below her was as deep and steep as a mountain canyon.

'I mustn't look down,' thought Colette, remembering the Death Tower again. The plastic bridge (she tried not to think of it as the Bridge of Doom) was in place now, but she was terrified that it would slip. She tested it with one foot and then the other. It felt firm enough – a lot firmer than her legs, which had suddenly started to wobble.

'Come on, 'Lette,' said Poppy. Colette could see her now, holding the bars of the cage and jumping up and down. Somehow the sight gave her strength, and before she knew it she had crossed the bridge and was on the dresser beside the cage. Poppy's delighted face and cry of ' 'Lette here!' were her reward.

Colette tried to reach the metal hook of the cage door, but it was just too high. She looked around the surface of the dresser for something she could use to yank it.

Near the cage was a giant ashtray and in it a match

as long as a human-size walking stick. Holding it above her head, she thrust it up against the hook.

Yes! The hook rose, the door swung open and Poppy ran out of the cage.

She flung herself at Colette like a puppy. Colette fell over backwards, with Poppy on top of her. They both laughed with the relief of being together again.

Then there was a clattering sound and they stopped laughing. The railway line had fallen to the floor.

'Bridge gone,' said Poppy.

They were stranded on the dresser.

This was too much to bear. Colette sat down and held her head in her hands.

'Have nice carrot,' suggested Poppy, trying to cheer her up.

Colette shook her head and shivered. Poppy went back into the cage and brought out her bedding: a knitted giant baby's sock and a giant handkerchief. She wrapped the handkerchief round Colette's shoulders.

'Nice warm sheet,' she said – and suddenly Colette knew what to do.

'Are there any more of these?' she asked.

Poppy dragged out four more handkerchiefs.

Colette wasn't an expert on knots like Stephen, but she thought she could remember how to tie a reef knot, even in the dark. Her fingers set to work.

Poppy realised immediately what she was doing.

'Go down sheets, go in garden, see Stephen,' she said.

'Yes,' said Colette.

'Take cosy bed too,' said Poppy, giving the sock a push. The matchstick fell down with it.

Colette was surprising herself with her knot-tying speed and skill. Soon all five handkerchiefs were tied together. She tied the top one to a bar of the cage and pushed the sheet ladder off the edge of the dresser. Would it be long enough? Yes – she could see that the last handkerchief was touching the kitchen floor.

'Like the Donkey,' said Poppy.

The Donkey was another climbing frame at the adventure playground. It had a tail made of knotted rope, which Poppy could confidently climb up and down. Remembering this stopped Colette feeling too nervous.

'I'll go first,' she said.

Hand over hand, she lowered herself to the floor. It was much quicker and less scary than climbing the vegetable rack had been.

Watching Poppy was worse, but Colette made herself remember the Donkey, and sure enough her little sister climbed down fearlessly and easily.

What a relief to be down on the ground again! At least, for Colette it was; Poppy was looking round the dim kitchen anxiously as if she expected the kitten to appear at any moment. Colette led her to the back door where the new cat-flap had been fitted.

'Too high,' said Poppy.

'It's all right – we can make a ramp with the railway line. I'll go and find it. Do you want to come with me?'

But Poppy was staring, horrified, at the cat-flap. Colette looked at it too, and had the impression it was moving slightly.

'Cat coming,' said Poppy in terror.

'Quick! Run!' Colette grabbed Poppy's hand and together they ran for the gap beside the fridge. They reached it safely and peeped out.

Yes, the cat-flap was definitely lifting slowly towards them. And now something was appearing from underneath it. Something pale and round. A face.

'Stephen!' shouted Poppy.

T HE LAWN MOWER stood waiting on the moonlit
path.

Stephen could guess exactly what Colette would say
when she saw what was in the trailer: 'Stephen Jones,
you've turned into a collector!' He tried out various
replies in his head.

But Colette didn't say it. In fact, it was all she could
do to climb into the trailer. He was shocked to see how
weak she seemed. She looked thin and dirty too.

'You're even more of a fright than I am,' he joked.

Colette smiled faintly, but all she said was, 'I'm so tired, Stephen. I just want to lie down.'

'Well, you can,' he told her, patting the giant gardening glove that filled up half the trailer. 'This bed's got compartments for all of us, and a couple to spare. And there's some thistledown inside that makes it quite cosy.'

Poppy, who didn't seem at all tired, helped him tuck Colette up in one of the fingers of the glove.

'I found it under the shed,' he said proudly. But Poppy was more impressed by the pile of giant blackberries as big as footballs.

'Help yourself,' he said, clambering into the driver's seat. He started the lawn mower up.

'All bumpy,' complained Poppy, as they jolted down the garden path.

'It's this gravel – it's like boulders,' said Stephen. 'It'll be smoother once we're on the road.'

And so it was. They drove through the night. Colette was asleep, and Poppy was too busy gorging herself on the juicy bobbles of the giant blackberries to talk much.

'Stephen have nice black'by?' she said at last, offering him one.

'No, I'm sick of them. They're just about all I've had to eat.'

They drove on in silence for a while. Then, 'Go to beanstalk, climb down?' asked Poppy.

'That's right,' said Stephen. But he was beginning to feel uneasy. He had been looking out for the buttons that Colette had dropped when they were captured, but he hadn't spotted any of them.

They came to a crossroads, and Stephen parked the lawn mower under an overhanging leaf. Which way now?

Colette woke up. After eating a whole blackberry she was more like her old self – annoyingly so.

'Stephen Jones, you've turned into a collector!' she said, exactly as he knew she would. As well as the glove, the blackberries and some extra thistledown, there was a stack of curly giant parsley and some garden nails as long as swords.

'Ah, but my collections are to keep us alive. I don't collect *useless* things.' He eyed the glittery bag which she had insisted on bringing with her.

'This is the running-away bag,' protested Colette. 'It's *full* of useful things.'

'Like food?' he asked hopefully.

'No,' admitted Colette. 'Well, there's a bit of carrot. We did have some other food, but we finished it all ages ago. Jumbeelia stopped feeding us, you see.'

'Big girl got snails,' explained Poppy.

'I expect she's gone off them too,' said Colette. 'None of her crazes seem to last very long.'

'That's the trouble with you stupid collectors,' said Stephen.

'So you think these are stupid then, do you?' Colette emptied the bag and produced his very own jeans and long-sleeved T-shirt.

'Cool! Where did you find these?' Stephen was already ripping off his thin torn floppy soldier's outfit.

'On the washing line Jumbeelia collected. We packed a sheet and a towel from it too. And look at these other things.'

Stephen inspected the giant items that Colette had tipped out of the bag. Three badges, three acorn cups, a few sweet papers, a matchstick, a baby's sock and some feathers.

'The badges are good,' he said, 'and I suppose the matchstick is OK.'

'It's more than OK,' said Colette. 'I opened Poppy's cage with it.'

'And that sock thing looks quite warm,' he admitted grudgingly. 'But why the feathers?'

Colette looked a bit sheepish then. 'Well, they don't weigh much,' she said. 'Anyway, you know what Poppy's like about feathers. She just fell in love with them.'

Typical, he thought. 'And I suppose she fell in love with these stupid acorn cups – or are they in aid of anything?'

'Get water?' suggested Poppy. It had been raining the day before, and she climbed down and filled one with water from a puddle.

'It doesn't look very clean,' said Colette, but they were too thirsty to worry about that. They ate another blackberry between them and nibbled some of the parsley, while Stephen told them all about his time outdoors – the days spent hiding and hunting for food, and the night-time searches for a way into the house.

'What about all the creepy crawlies?' asked Colette.

'I think most of them were more frightened of me than I was of them. The worst thing was that cat – always nosing around under the shed.'

'Naughty cat,' said Poppy, looking around as if she half-expected it to be coming down the road.

But the road was empty, although the sky was light by now.

'Hadn't we better be going?' asked Colette.

'Yes, but which way? I haven't found any of your famous buttons yet.'

'We might now that it's daytime. Why don't we each look down a different road?'

Stephen agreed, but he searched with a heavy heart. He had a horrible feeling they might have gone the wrong way in the first place.

Poppy treated the button-hunt as a party game. 'I find flower! I find stick!' she shouted, and then, extra loud, 'I find poo poo!'

'Well, don't tread on it!' Stephen shouted back.

'Little poo poo. Baa Lamb poo poo!' said Poppy.

Stephen and Colette came to look.

'They're probably from a giant mouse,' said Colette.

'No – I know what those look like,' said Stephen, whose time in the garden had turned him into something of an expert. 'These ones *do* look like sheep droppings – normal sheep, I mean, not giant ones.'

'But Jumbeelia's mother put the sheep down the . . .' Colette stopped, but Poppy couldn't hear her anyway. She had wandered a bit further down her road, and she now called out, 'More poo poo!'

'We may as well go that way,' said Stephen, and they climbed back into the lawn mower.

They followed the trail of droppings for a mile or so. Then, 'I'm sure the beanstalk wasn't this far away,' said Colette. 'Shouldn't we go back, Stephen?'

'We can't. We're nearly out of petrol.'

Almost as if the lawn mower heard him, its engine noise spluttered and then died, and they came to a stop.

'Oh no,' said Colette. 'We'll have to walk.'

'Don't want to walk,' said Poppy.

'You wimpy woodlice,' said Stephen, but his heart wasn't really in insulting them. He was too worried.

Suddenly he felt very tired. He hadn't slept all night. Neither had Poppy. Colette was better rested, but she still seemed very weak.

Still, there was no choice. The girls realised it too. They wrapped a few of the firmest blackberries in sweet papers, and stuffed them into the bag, along with the nails and some of the thistledown. Colette shouldered the bag wearily, while Stephen dragged the glove-bed behind him.

As they trudged along the road he couldn't resist a glance back at the lawn mower. He hated leaving it there. He had been cherishing a wild hope that he could somehow get it safely down the beanstalk.

To his surprise, he could only just see it. It was shrouded in mist. Stephen realised that the air around them was growing thick, cold and white.

'This feels right,' said Colette.

And then, without warning, the road just stopped. In front of them was an enormous stone wall.

'What do we do now?' asked Stephen.

'Go through hole,' said Poppy, pointing to a gap between some of the lowest stones.

The other side of the giant wall, the mist was thicker still. 'Let's hold hands,' said Colette.

The ground was bare and slippery and the air cold and clammy. They shuffled forwards together.

'If you were a giant you wouldn't even be able to see the ground,' said Stephen.

'I can, though,' said Colette, 'and I can see a button!' She picked it up triumphantly. 'So we *are* on the right track!'

Just then, they heard a muffled bleating.

'Baa Lamb!' shouted Poppy. She broke free and started to run.

'Stop! You might fall off the edge!' Stephen caught up with her, grabbed her elbow and slowed her down.

The bleating came again, and at the same time the mist thinned slightly and they all saw Baa Lamb. He was standing at the very edge of the land, gazing out into the empty space beyond. He looked tattier than ever. The end of one of his twisty horns had broken off, and his wool was full of bits and pieces, as if he had been rolling about in a giant compost heap.

'Baa Lamb!' Poppy cried again, reaching out to him.

The sheep remained still, gazing down, and Stephen thought he had a forlorn look about him.

'And look, another button!' exclaimed Colette. 'So the beanstalk must be just here.'

But it wasn't.

The spy

Comings and goings. Goings and comings. Throg had been keeping a watchful eye on the policeman's house, and it was all very suspicious.

First the boy had gone away. A day or so later the old lady had arrived and the mother had gone away. And then, yesterday evening, the boy had come back again, accompanied by an old man. What did it all mean? Throg felt sure that in some mysterious way this family was in league with the iggly plops. Most likely

The Giants and the Joneses

the whole police force was involved too.

Throg crept up to the front door. He could hear raised voices inside the house. One of them seemed to be crying and shrieking. Throg's hearing wasn't as good as his eyesight, but he was convinced he heard the words 'iggly plop'.

He knocked at the door. He knew that if he asked the usual question he would get the usual answer, so he decided he would try and catch them out. Instead of asking if they had seen any iggly plops he would ask them *how many* they had seen.

The policeman opened the door. Throg recognised him even though he wasn't wearing his uniform.

'Heek munchly iggly plops?' he asked.

The man seemed to hesitate – a sure sign of guilt. Then, as he opened his mouth to speak, the girl charged out of a room. Her face looked swollen and tear-stained, and in her hand she carried a string of knotted handkerchiefs.

'Nug!' she shouted. 'Nug iggly plops! Glay awook!'

The father put an arm round the girl, but she wriggled it off and ran upstairs. The man shrugged apologetically. 'Yimp,' he said to Throg, and closed the door.

Throg hovered on the pavement, uncertain what to do, and then a picture flashed into his mind. It was a picture of the back garden, on the day that he had spoken to the old lady. He could see the scene quite clearly: he was leaning over the garden gate, and the old lady had left her knitting on a chair to come and talk to him. The girl was there too, and a black spratchkin which had jumped out of her arms and run to the garden shed. All the time that Throg and the old lady had been talking, the spratchkin had been poking about under the shed. That must be where the iggly plops were hiding!

Clutching his can of weedkiller, Throg hobbled down the lane at the side of the house. He opened the gate and crept into the back garden. There was the shed – and there, on his knees, reaching under it with a stick, was the boy.

Hearing Throg's feet crunching on the gravel, the boy turned round. He was grinning.

Throg came straight out with his new question:

'Heek munchly iggly plops?' and this time he got a different answer.

'Thrink,' said the boy, holding out three fingers as if Throg was an idiot. Then a cunning look came into his face, and he asked if there was a reward for finding them and handing them over.

Of course there was a reward! 'Sprubbin!' Throg told him. The reward for giving up the iggly plops would be joy – the joy of having freed Groil from the wicked creatures who were planning to destroy it.

But the boy didn't seem interested in that kind of reward. He had lost interest in poking around under the shed too, dropping his stick, he made a rude sign at Throg and went into the house.

Never mind. Throg knew where they were now, and he was certain there were more than three of them. There was probably a whole army under there.

He unscrewed the top of his can, in readiness; then he lowered his old body to the ground. Lying on his tummy, he peered under the shed.

Nothing. Nothing except a few cobwebs and a couple of blackberries. They had got away, the rascals! Or they had been hidden away.

As Throg heaved himself back to his feet, he heard someone opening the back door of the house. At the same time, he noticed that the shed door was open a crack. Before he could be spotted he slipped inside.

Peeping through the crack, he saw the girl come out of the house. He noticed that she was carrying a small wooden box. Halfway down the garden path she paused and looked over her shoulder, as if she was afraid someone might be following her.

And someone soon would be following her! Throg was just about to creep out of the shed and go after her himself when he heard more footsteps on the path.

It was the boy again. Like the girl, he had a secretive air about him. When he reached the garden gate he stopped, peered over it and then waited for a few minutes before opening it.

Was he stalking his sister, spying on her? Or was it just a game?

If so, it was a game which Throg could play too.

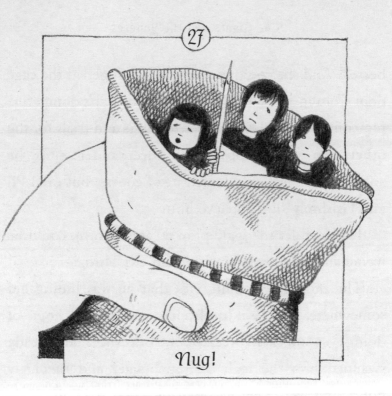

Nug!

Tears blinded Jumbeelia's eyes as she ran along the road towards the edgeland. Her feet tapped out an angry rhythm: *Zab ez frikely, Zab ez frikely.*

Why couldn't her horrible brother have stayed with Grishpij for ever instead of coming back home and messing up her life again? What had he done with the iggliest plop?

Jumbeelia didn't believe for a moment that the tiny girl had knotted those handkerchiefs together all by herself. And she couldn't possibly have opened the cage door from inside. The whole thing was Zab's doing. She remembered how he loved setting tests and trials for the other two iggly plops. This sheet-ladder must be another of those. Zab denied it, of course, but even Pij and Grishmij didn't believe him.

Had Zab let the iggly plop escape? Worse, could he have handed her over to that mad old Throg?

The most likely thing was that he was hiding her somewhere, to tease Jumbeelia, and in the hope of doing yet another sweefswoof. But she had already swapped him the iggly strimpchogger and the iggly pobo, and she knew he wasn't interested in the iggly frangle because it didn't work. There were no other iggly gadgets left in Jumbeelia's collection. Her only hope was to climb down the bimplestonk again in search of some items which might appeal to Zab.

That is, if the bimplestonk was still there. She had heard old Throg chanting about how he had kraggled it. Just in case he really had, Jumbeelia had brought the box of bimples. They rattled gently in time to her footsteps: *Zab ez frikely, Zab ez frikely, Zab ez . . .*

Crash! The rhythm stopped abruptly as Jumbeelia stumbled over something and fell.

She had grazed her knee slightly, but far more interesting than the droplets of blood was the object which had tripped her up. It was the iggly strimpchogger.

So Zab had been here! What was he doing so near the edgeland? Could he have taken the iggly plop there?

A new and horrible fear filled Jumbeelia's mind as she picked up the strimpchogger and continued on her way.

She clambered over the wall into the edgeland. The mist swirled around her as she inched her way forward over the slippery rocks towards the emptiness.

A reddish boulder loomed out of the mist. She noticed that there were some words scratched on the stone in uneven capital letters:

ISH EZ QUEESH THROG KRAGGLED
O BIMPLESTONK.

So old Throg had carved these ragged letters. And perhaps he really had killed the bimplestonk too, as the writing boasted, because here she was at the very edge of the land, and there was no sign of it.

Jumbeelia peered out into the emptiness, and reached out too. Nothing. No stalk, no leaves, no pods full of bimples.

And then she saw it. Not the bimplestonk, but the glove – an old gardening glove, lying at the foot of the boulder.

Jumbeelia picked the glove up, and then nearly dropped it in shock when it spoke to her.

'Put us down!' it said.

Jumbeelia peeped into the glove and there, peeping back at her from one of the fingers, was the boy iggly plop. He was waving a nail and looking fierce.

Jumbeelia saw that the other two were there as well, tucked inside two more fingers. How *could* Zab have just left them there like that?

Never mind – they were safe now. She spoke to them reassuringly, telling them that she would take them back home, get Pij to build them a newer, bigger, cage, and that she wouldn't let Zab or the spratchkin get them, not ever again. She would put them in her collecting bag now and take them straight back home . . .

'Nug!' a voice interrupted her.

It wasn't the boy this time. It wasn't the wild girl either. It was the iggliest one, and it was speaking to her in Groilish!

'Nug, Jumbeelia. Glay jum, boff bimplestonk.'

Over the edge

'GLAY JUM, BOFF bimplestonk,' repeated Poppy. Colette could hardly believe what she was hearing. Her little sister, who couldn't even speak English properly, was talking away to a giant. And Jumbeelia was answering her. They were having a proper conversation.

When Colette thought back, it began to make sense. Poppy had spent nearly a week on her own with Jumbeelia. And more recently, in the cage, she had been chatted to every day in giant language – not just by Jumbeelia but by her father and grandmother.

Although Colette couldn't understand the words, she could read the expressions on Jumbeelia's face. The girl giant looked puzzled at first, and then a little disappointed.

'What was all that gobbledygook?' Stephen asked.

'I saying go home down beanstalk,' said Poppy.

'What beanstalk?' Stephen sounded like his old irritable self, but Poppy wasn't put out. 'Big girl got beans,' she said.

Jumbeelia started spouting some more giant language. Colette didn't think she sounded happy at all.

'What's she saying now?'

'Big girl saying she likes us. She's got nice house.'

'Tell her we want to see our mum and dad again.'

'Oggle woor mij twerko, oggle woor pij tweeko,' Poppy pleaded with Jumbeelia.

Jumbeelia seemed to understand at last. Her face cleared, and she lowered the glove gently down to the ground.

The three children scrambled out. Jumbeelia

squatted beside them, and Colette saw that she was holding a box, made of different shapes of painted wood. She was fiddling about with it, as if she was searching for something on its surface, a hidden lever or panel. Suddenly a drawer in the box sprang open. She lowered it so they could all see the squirly wrinkled round things inside.

'Bimples,' she said.

'Big girl saying beans,' said Poppy.

'Obviously,' said Stephen, but he couldn't guess Jumbeelia's meaning when she then announced, 'Bimplestonk chingulay.'

'Beanstalk tomorrow,' Poppy translated proudly.

'She's going to throw one of them over the edge,' said Colette. 'That must be how the last beanstalk sprang up.'

A warm feeling of relief spread through her whole body. Bean today, beanstalk tomorrow. Just one more day! That wasn't long to wait. And now Jumbeelia was on their side!

She looked up gratefully and saw that Jumbeelia was smiling down at her. Suddenly the girl giant felt like a real friend.

Jumbeelia reached into the box to pick up a bean.

At the same time, a figure emerged from the mist and they heard a voice.

'Wahoy!'

Colette's relief chilled into terror. It was Zab.

'Quick! Hide!' yelled Stephen. He took Poppy's hand and pulled her behind the carved boulder. Colette ran after them, but she was too late. Zab had spotted her. She heard his leering laugh, and the next moment his fingers were curled around her body, squeezing her and lifting her up in the air.

And now he was stretching his arm, reaching out into the cold mist beyond the edge of the land.

He wouldn't really do it, surely? He wouldn't throw her off? He was just trying to wind up his sister, wasn't he? Colette's heart beat furiously.

'Wunk, rwunk, thrink . . .'

She felt his grip loosen.

'Askorp!' came Jumbeelia's voice suddenly.

The grip tightened again. Colette saw that the girl giant was standing beside her brother, and that she too was dangling something over the edge of Giant Land.

It was the lawn mower!

'Nug! Osh ez *mub* strimpchogger,' cried Zab.

'Osh ez *mub* iggly plop,' replied Jumbeelia, and Colette realised that Zab was being forced to choose between her life and the loss of the lawn mower.

Zab hesitated. Slowly, he lowered Colette – then stuffed her into his trouser pocket while he lunged for the lawn mower. Colette peered out fearfully and saw him try to wrest it from Jumbeelia's grasp.

They were struggling now, locked together in serious combat. Colette lost her grip on the edge of the pocket and slipped down inside it.

In the crushing darkness she was swung this way and that, till there came an enormous jolt, and she heard Stephen shout, 'Quick, Colette! Climb out! They're on the ground.'

Colette managed to wriggle her way out of the pocket into the pale chilly daylight. She slid down Zab's thigh on to the rocky ground.

Stephen was there, waiting. He caught her hand and tugged her behind the rock. There was Poppy, and the sheep, who was eating their supply of parsley, completely unaware of the crisis.

The children peered round the boulder and saw the two giants wrestling. They saw Zab tug the lawn mower free from Jumbeelia's hands. They saw him break away from her with a jerk which sent her rolling in the other direction.

And they saw her slip over the edge.

'No! Nug! Help big girl! Aheesh!' cried out Poppy. She ran forward.

'Come back, Poppy!'

All of them froze, aghast at the sight of Jumbeelia, who was clinging to a ridge of rock with the fingers of both hands. Her body was dangling over the edge of the land.

Zab looked aghast too. He was kneeling beside her, clutching one arm and trying to pull her back to safety. But he wasn't strong enough. Now Jumbeelia had lost her hold on the rock, and was dangling in Zab's grip.

'If he doesn't let go she'll pull him over too,' said Stephen.

'Aheesh! Aheesh!' shouted Zab at the top of his voice.

'Ee aheesh! I help!' cried Poppy, but Stephen held

her back, and Colette said gently, 'We can't help. We're too small.'

'No one can help them now,' said Stephen.

29

Oidle oy

'AHEESH! AHEESH!' IT was the boy's voice. He sounded desperate.

Throg unscrewed the cap of his can of weedkiller again and tottered towards the cry for help.

A terrible sight met his eyes. The boy was leaning over the edge of the land, into the misty emptiness, and both his hands were clamped around his sister's arm, which looked as if it was nearly out of its socket. The girl was hanging in the emptiness. Any second now the

· 173 ·

boy would lose his grip and she would fall.

The boy turned a terrified white face towards Throg. 'Aheesh!' he whispered hoarsely.

The girl's other arm was flailing about wildly. Throg knelt down, reached out and caught hold of it. As he did so he felt his knees slipping towards the edge. The girl was surprisingly heavy, and for one dizzy moment Throg thought she would take him with her, crashing down to the land of the iggly plops. What a way to die!

But then he caught the desperate hope in the girl's eyes and he knew he had to rescue her. If they pulled together they could do it.

'Wunk, twunk, thrink, haroof!' he croaked.

The girl's head rose above the rocky edge of the land. Her shoulders followed.

'Tweeko!'

With a supreme effort they pulled again until her tummy was on the rock and she was wriggling herself forward to safety.

The boy let go then. He looked even whiter than before, ghostly white. Instead of lingering to comfort his sister or thank Throg he grabbed something – a toy car, was it? – and ran.

The girl was sitting up now, hunched over, her arms wrapped around herself, shaking. Still kneeling, Throg patted her head awkwardly and murmured, 'Ootle rootle.'

And then his eye lit on something and he stopped patting and telling her it was all right, because it wasn't. It wasn't ootle rootle at all.

There on the ground lay an open box, and the box was full of bimples!

In an instant Throg was on his feet, the can in his hand, sloshing the poisonous liquid over the beans.

'Nug! Nug kraggle o bimples!' shouted the girl.

And from behind the boulder – *his* boulder, the one he had carved – there rushed a tiny ferocious figure. It wagged its finger at him.

'Pecky, pecky, pecky!' it scolded.

An iggly plop, and one who could speak Groilish!

The can was still in Throg's hand. He tilted it towards the horrible creature.

At the same time, something stung one of his toes.

He lifted his foot, wobbled, and sat down with a thump. The can went flying from his hand. It must have been almost empty because not a drop spilt from it as it bounced, once, twice, and then disappeared over the edge.

'Yes!' came an iggly triumphant voice from the ground.

It was the toe-stinger – an iggly plop, wearing a round shield and armed with a nail. Beside him stood two more, one with its arm round the other. Throg recognised the iggliest one as the finger-wagger.

Looking more closely, he was amazed to see that they were only children.

He reached out for them, but the girl giant was too quick for him. She had scooped them up.

'Beely iggly plops!' she said. At least, that's what he thought she said, but he was distracted by another sound. A long loud bleat.

A grubby, tatty-looking fleecy creature had appeared from behind the boulder. Although it had splendid curly horns it had a needy, pathetic air about it. It looked up at Throg plaintively with its beely yellowish eyes and bleated again.

Throg's heart melted. He picked the creature up and held it to his withered old cheek. The familiar, comforting smell of dirty wool filled his nostrils.

He looked down at the iggly plops in the girl's hands, suddenly feeling baffled.

She understood his look, and seemed to want to explain things to him.

'O iggly plops ev niffled oy o iggly blebber,' she said.

Could he be hearing right? Could the three iggly plop children really have given him this adorable woolly creature?

In a flash, Throg saw it all. Tears of gratitude filled his eyes. These three miniature children were on his side. They had rebelled against their terrible tribe. They had climbed the bimplestonk just for him. They had given him back his Lolshly!

'Oidle oy! Oidle oy, iggly plops!' he murmured

Unpicking the stitches

'GIVE BACK! NIFFLE abreg!' Poppy was clamouring for the return of Baa Lamb.

The old giant didn't appear to hear her; he was too busy stroking and talking to the sheep, who had stopped bleating and seemed to be enjoying the attention.

'I think Baa Lamb likes the old giant,' Colette said.

But Poppy wasn't convinced. 'Baa Lamb go home,' she kept repeating.

Stephen did his best to reason with her. 'Think,

Poppy. What happens to sheep back home? We eat them. Whereas this old guy obviously wants this one as a pet. I think we should let him keep Baa Lamb.'

'Baa Lamb go home down beanstalk,' said Poppy stubbornly.

Stephen's patience, which Colette had been admiring, broke.

'*What* beanstalk?' he snapped. 'There isn't a beanstalk, you silly little larva. And now there won't be. All Jumbo's beans have been poisoned.'

Poppy looked disappointed, but then her face cleared. 'Fly down with feathers,' she said.

'Could we, Stephen?' asked Colette. 'Could we make ourselves some wings? Strap the giant feathers to our arms somehow?'

'It wouldn't work,' he said in his Mr Know-All voice. 'We wouldn't be able to keep our arms apart. We're not like birds – our muscles aren't strong enough. We'd just go down like bullets.'

Poppy couldn't understand the science but she got the message and began to cry.

'Roopy iggly plop,' murmured Jumbeelia. She put

them all down gently, then reached into her pocket and pulled out a handkerchief.

And another one. And another one. Five handkerchiefs, all knotted together.

'Look! They're the sheets from your cage, Poppy!' said Colette.

'Climb down sheets, go home,' said Poppy, sniffing, as Jumbeelia dabbed her eyes with a corner of one of the giant handkerchiefs.

'It's much too far,' said Colette. 'I expect we'd need about five *thousand* sheets for that.' She glanced at Stephen, half expecting him to pour scorn on her calculations.

'What about the harnesses, though?' he muttered to himself.

'What are you talking about?'

Stephen was staring at the sheet-handkerchiefs in a kind of trance.

'Stephen?'

'Parachutes,' he said.

Suddenly she understood.

'You mean we can use the giant hankies to parachute

back home? That's a brilliant idea!'

But Stephen hadn't quite convinced himself yet. 'The trouble is, we'd have to make harnesses for our bodies, and then somehow tie the hankies on to them. We really need some rope and some cords.'

'How about the sock?' suggested Colette. 'The one Poppy slept in when she was in the cage.'

She fetched it from the running-away bag, made a hole in it with one of the nails, and started to unravel the wool.

Jumbeelia didn't look happy. She seemed to be telling them off, and Poppy translated. 'Big girl saying sock for baby.'

'Tell her we're making parachute harnesses,' said Stephen, but Poppy didn't know these words in English, let alone in giant language.

'We're going to fly down with the hankies,' Colette explained, holding her arms up to mime a parachute, and Poppy translated for Jumbeelia.

The giant wool, strong and thick but soft, was just right for the harnesses, and Stephen – who had read countless books about pilots bailing out of burning planes – knew how to wind it round their bodies and what sort of knots to tie. Meanwhile, Jumbeelia helped Colette to undo the handkerchiefs.

Old Throg, still cuddling Baa Lamb – or Lolshly, as he insisted on calling him – looked on with bright-eyed interest.

'Iggly plops glay jum,' he said approvingly.

'Old man saying us go home,' said Poppy.

But Stephen was frowning again.

'This wool is good for the harnesses, but we really need something thinner for the parachute cords,' he said.

'I know! The running-away bag!' exclaimed Colette.

The bag was harder to unravel than the sock had been, but the glittery thread from which it was woven was just the right thickness for parachute cords, and before long they had enough of it to attach to the corners of the handkerchiefs and to their harnesses.

'It's a pity we haven't got any crash helmets,' said Stephen.

'I've already thought of that,' said Colette. Proudly, she produced the three acorn cups from the running-away collection.

'Hat,' said Poppy, putting one on her head.

Jumbeelia clapped her hands. She was clearly pleased that one of her collections was being put to good use.

Colette knew the feeling. 'See?' she felt like saying to Stephen, but she stopped herself.

'Yahaw! Yahaw! Bye bye, big girl,' Poppy was saying now. She had climbed on to Jumbeelia's shoe and was clasping her ankle in a goodbye hug.

Gently, the girl giant picked her up and lifted her towards her mouth.

Colette remembered the first time Jumbeelia had done this. So long ago it seemed! They had feared then that she was going to eat them. This time they knew what was in store.

'The sooner this is over the better,' said Stephen, bracing himself for his goodbye kiss. At least this time he didn't say 'Yuk' when it happened.

And now it was Colette's turn. The giant kiss seemed even wetter than the usual ones, till Colette realised that some of the wetness was salty and came from the tears which were trickling down Jumbeelia's cheeks.

With a sudden rush of pity for the girl giant, Colette almost wished she could promise, 'We'll be back.' But even if she had been able to say it in giant language, it wouldn't be true. Instead, she shyly said, 'Yahaw,' as Poppy had done.

Jumbeelia smiled through her tears and put Colette carefully back on the ground beside the other two. Poppy was now waving up at the old giant and the sheep.

'Yahaw, floopy plop! Yahaw, iggly blebber!' she said.

'That's enough, Poppy – we don't want *him* to start slobbering over us,' said Stephen. But there was no danger of that. The old giant took a nervous step back, still holding Baa Lamb firmly to his cheek as if he was half afraid that they might reclaim the creature. He muttered 'Yahaw,' and waggled the fingers of his other hand, but more in a 'be off with you' kind of gesture than a proper wave.

And it *was* time to be off. Off the edge and down through the clouds. Poppy was already standing there, poised for the plunge.

'No, Poppy. I'll go first,' said Stephen. 'Then you,

and then Colette.' Although he was taking charge, his voice sounded a little shaky, and Colette saw that his hands were shaking too as he raised them above his head.

'Watch me, and do what I do,' he told them. 'Arms up, legs apart, head back. Then lean forward. Like this.'

He leaned forward. He jumped.

He was gone, swallowed up by the cloud.

'Wunk, twunk, thrink, boff!' Poppy was gone too.

Colette stood on the edge of Giant Land, in the very spot where Zab had dangled her. Then she had been sick with fear. Her fear now was mixed with a wild excitement.

Her mind raced forward – she was landing, she was running home across the fields with Stephen and Poppy, they were hugging Mum and Dad, they were telling everyone about their adventures.

'It won't happen unless I jump,' she said to her pounding heart. And she jumped.

She plummeted through the clouds. The wind roaring in her ears was almost deafening. Such speed, such noise! She had never felt anything like this before.

And then there was a terrific jerk, and the roaring noise stopped.

The mist had cleared. Colette looked up. The handkerchief, full of air, billowed above her. She looked down. Two tiny figures drifted below her.

She was floating. She was free.

Three years later

'BEESH, BEESH, *BEESH*, Jumbeelia!' the girl giant pleaded. She was sitting up in bed and gazing at her big sister.

Their mother pottered about the room, tidying up and half-listening to the story she had heard her older daughter tell so many times before. It was a ridiculous story, she thought, but anything was better than the awful books she used to have to read to Jumbeelia. Thank goodness she didn't have to go through all that with Woozly.

Jumbeelia sat on Woozly's bed. Both pairs of eyes were alight as Jumbeelia told the story she never tired of telling and Woozly never tired of hearing. This story didn't come out of a book. It was the story of Jumbeelia and the iggly plops.

English/Groilish Dictionary

again – tweeko

all – ootle

and – da

are – oor

around – arump

away – awook

baby – bobbaleely

back – abreg

bad – pecky

bean – bimple

beanstalk – bimplestonk

button – whackleclack

cat – spratch

chip – snishsnosh

cuddly – woozly

cushions – squodgies

down – boff

drink – gloosh

father – pij

fill – whedderwhay

funny – heehuckerly

Giant Land – Groil

giant language – Groilish

give – niffle

go – glay

goodbye – yahaw

grandfather – grishpij

grandmother – grishmij

grass – strimp

grow – eep

have – ev

heart – jarn

hello – wahoy

help – ahcesh

home – jum

horrible – frikely

how – heek

I – ee

I'll – eel

is – ez

joy – sprubbin

kill – kraggle

killer – kraggler

kind – jin

kitten – spratchkin

land – chay

lawn mower – strimpchogger

little – iggly

look – oggle

lovely – beely

many – munchly

mine – mubbin

mother – mij

my – mub

naughty – pecky

no – nug

not – nug

old – floopy

one – wunk

other – ithry

our – woor

peace – zab

person – plop

phone – frangle

pillar box – pobo

please – beesh

poor – roopy

pound – poddum

pull – haroof

quickly – flisterflay

right – rootle

see – oggle

sheep – blebber

sorry – yimp

splash – glishglursh

stop – askorp

swap – sweefswoof

thank you – oidle oy

that – osh

the – o

them – uth

they – uth

this – ish

three – thrink

tomorrow – chingulay

two – twunk

weed – veep

weedkiller – veep kraggler

warning – throg

washing line – swisheroo

where – queesh

white – lolshly

with – fa

worm – squerple

you – oy

Groilish/English Dictionary

abreg – back

aheesh – help

arump – around

askorp – stop

awook – away

beely – lovely

beesh – please

bimple – bean

bimplestonk – beanstalk

blebber – sheep

bobbaleely – baby

boff – down

chay – land

chingulay – tomorrow

da – and

ee – I

eel – I'll

eep – grow

eeped – grown

ev – have

ez – is

fa – with

flisterflay – quickly

floopy – old

frangle – phone

frikely – horrible

frimmot – carrot

glay – go

glishglursh – splash

gloosh – drink

grishmij – grandmother

grishpij – grandfather

Groil – Giant Land

Groilish – giant language

haroof – pull

heehuckerly – funny

heek – how

iggly – little

· 195 ·

ish – this
ithry – other
jarn – heart
jin – kind
jum – home
kraggle – kill
kraggler – killer
lolshly – white
mij – mother
mub – my
mubbin – mine
munchly – many
niffle – give
nug – no, not
o – the
oggle – look, see
oggled – seen
oidle oy – thank you
oor – are
ootle – all
osh – that
oy – you

pecky – bad, naughty
pij – father
plop – person
pobo – pillar box
poddum – pound
queesh – where
roopy – poor
rootle – right
snishsnosh – chip
spratch – cat
spratchkin – kitten
sprubbin – joy
squerple – worm
squodgies – cushions
strimp – grass
strimpchogger – lawn
  mower
sweefswoof – swap
swisheroo – washing line
thrink – three
throg – warning
tweeko – again

twunk – two

uth – they, them

veep – weed

veep kraggler – weedkiller

wahoy – hello

whackleclack – button

whedderwhay – fill

woor – our

woozly – cuddly

wunk – one

yahaw – goodbye

yimp – sorry

zab – peace

Julia Donaldson, the 2011-2013 Children's Laureate, is the outrageously talented, prize-winning author of the world's most-loved picture books including *The Gruffalo*, *What the Ladybird Heard*, *Stickman*, *The Scarecrows' Wedding* and *Night Monkey, Day Monkey*. Julia Donaldson's collaborations with Axel Scheffler have sold millions of copies, and *Room on the Broom* is now an Academy Award-nominated short film.